THE INTERPLANETARY EXPEDITION OF

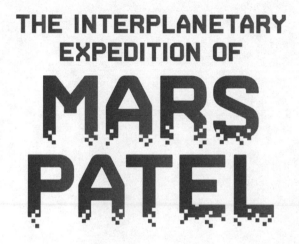

MARS PATEL

SHEELA CHARI

Based on the podcast series created by
BENJAMIN STROUSE
CHRIS TARRY
DAVID KREIZMAN
& JENNY TURNER HALL

WALKER BOOKS

THE INTERPLANETARY EXPEDITION OF
MARS PATEL

FOR KEERTHANA

15 ▶ 30 ╷╷╷╷╷╷╷╷╷╷╷╷╷╷╷╷╷╷╷╷╷╷

Hey, podcast listeners,
Oliver Pruitt here.
Welcome to a different journey!

With all great adventure comes great risk,
but I believe in the future I'm building,
especially with Mars Patel on the way!

Happy LANDING, but do be careful.
That first step is a doozy . . .

To the stars!

1100 Comments ⊗

staryoda   38 min ago
did OP kidnap mars??

allie_j   33 min ago
maybe OP & Mars r the same person

galaxygenius   26 min ago

no way mars is human OP is not

lostinlondon   15 min ago

OP is human and he's saving your idiot planet

he's saving us all

1

WELCOME TO ZERO GRAVITY

When Mars dreamed of traveling to distant planets, vomit wasn't the first thing that came to mind. But here he was hurtling through space on the *Pruitt 3*, hurling into a barf bag.

"Mars, say goodbye to Earth! You are about to go on the adventure of your life!" crowed Oliver Pruitt, the billionaire inventor who had orchestrated this journey on his own spaceship. Of course, he wasn't *actually* in the cockpit. Only a hologram version of him stood there. But that didn't stop the man from gushing virtually from his control center millions of miles away. "Go on, float around," Oliver called out as Mars turned green. "Welcome to zero gravity!"

Just a few minutes ago, after leaving Earth, Mars had unbuckled his harness and felt himself free-floating inside the walls of the cockpit, somersaulting and pinwheeling his way through the cabin. First he was right side up, then he was upside down until his limbs felt like clouds, and the universe zoomed by outside in a veil of darkness. Was this really happening to him? Was he really on a spaceship headed to the planet Mars?

Meanwhile, Oliver Pruitt watched, looking sharp in his maroon space suit. Mars wasn't even sure when Oliver had changed. Back on Earth, he had appeared to Mars and his friends in a muted white flight suit. Now Mars's friends and his mom were left behind, maybe forever. It had been twelve minutes since liftoff, but to Mars, it felt like a lifetime. He needed to know where Aurora was, and why Oliver had led him to outer space, far from everyone Mars loved.

But first Mars had other problems. He heaved into the paper bag.

"I think I just barfed up a lung," he said weakly.

"Nothing like traveling through space for the first time! What you're feeling, Mars, is motion sickness as your body adjusts to weightlessness. But don't worry. You'll get used it in no time. And then the fun really begins!"

The door to the cockpit burst open.

"Mr. Pruitt, we've got a problem," announced a girl in an orange flight suit who had tumbled into the room. She was small-boned with a slightly upturned nose and a cascade of dark brown curls floating around her square face.

Mars stared in disbelief. "You're Lost in London! I mean, you're Julia!" He recognized her immediately from the missing-children flyers he and his friends had found back in Port Elizabeth. But where had she come from? Had she been on the spacecraft the entire time? "When did you get here?" he asked.

Julia rolled her eyes at him but her voice was gentle. "Mars, I didn't *get* here, I've *been* here. But honestly, I don't have time to explain when we're in an emergency. Mr. Pruitt, I need to know if—"

But hologram Oliver Pruitt was fading away.

Julia's eyebrows knitted together. "Mr. Pruitt!" she repeated crossly.

"Sorry, Julia! Have to run! But it sounds like you've got it under control!" Oliver Pruitt was growing fainter and fainter until he was just a shimmer.

"Wait! Don't go!" Mars cried out. "You need to answer my questions. Where's Aurora? What's going to happen to my friends and my mom? And why did you lie to me? Why did you make us go through all of that on Earth?"

"That's a lot of questions," Oliver said wryly.

"I need to know!"

"I had to make sure you were ready for the Red Planet." Oliver now was barely an outline. "Wait until you get here. The Colony will blow your mind!"

"Colony?" Mars repeated. "Is that where Aurora is?"

"There's so much to tell you, Mars. About why I chose you for the mission. Because you are—"

The spaceship lurched horribly.

"WARNING: BREACH IMMINENT IN SECTOR C." The announcement rang across the speakers, followed by an alarm.

"Mr. Pruitt!" Julia said again, more urgently. But Oliver Pruitt had vanished from the cockpit. "Oh, great! Just what we need. A commander-in-chief who's MIA."

"WARNING: BREACH IMMINENT IN SECTOR C."

The alarm sounded again, and Mars felt like his life was repeating. Wasn't it just a few weeks ago that he and Caddie were hiding out in a janitor closet at school during a Code Red? Were alarms going to follow him his whole life—even in space?

"Is that warning serious?" Mars asked nervously. "What does it mean?"

Julia had floated to an intercom mounted on the wall and now said loudly into the mic, "We need you on the flight deck—NOW!" Then she turned to Mars. "It means that if we don't do something about that hole in Sector C, we're going to burn up like a marshmallow on an open flame. Which is what I was trying to tell Oliver Pruitt before he vanished on us."

"WARNING: CATASTROPHIC BREACH IN SECTOR C.

CATASTROPHIC BREACH IN SECTOR C. ALL SYSTEMS
DISENGAGE IN THREE MINUTES."

"Does that mean we're going to die?" Mars felt his heart
thud. Until now it had seemed like things were going
well enough. Sure, he'd thought Pruitt Prep was a normal
school on Gale Island, until he found out that it was also
a spacecraft heading to Mars. And sure, Oliver had tricked
him into coming on board, but Mars hadn't expected to die
on the man's watch.

Now Oliver was gone. And catastrophe was around the
corner.

"It means we have to handle this problem ourselves,"
Julia said. "That means *you*, Mars."

"But I d-don't—" Mars stuttered in a panic. "I've never
been on a spaceship, and I never—"

Julia steeled herself. "I get it. This is all new for you. It's
natural to freak out. But I need you to calm down so you
can help us not die. You think you can handle that?"

Behind Julia, a panel slid open. A teenage guy in a gray
flight suit floated in. His brown eyes were wide-spaced and
intelligent, and he looked like he hadn't had a haircut in
weeks. "Places, everybody," he said easily. "These interplanetary space shuttles don't fly themselves."

Mars stared at him, agog. Who else was on board this
spaceship?

"You really took forever, Orion," Julia said. "We have less than three minutes."

Orion tumbled toward the cockpit and slipped into the pilot seat. He strapped himself in next to Julia, who was already strapped and waiting for him. "I heard, I heard," he said to her. He inputted some numbers into the control panel. "Julia, you handle the throttle."

"Roger that."

Orion turned to Mars. "How about you, Butterfly?" he said evenly.

"Butterfly?" Mars repeated. "Wait, who are you?"

"Mars, Orion, Orion, Mars," Julia said, making quick introductions. "He's the pilot."

"Think you can spin us?" Orion pointed to a wheel mounted on a console behind them.

"I guess," Mars said unsurely.

"That will mean you aren't buckled in, OK?" Orion asked. "So hold on tight, or you're really going to be flying around here like a butterfly. Start turning that wheel. Now!"

The wheel was surprisingly heavy. Mars gripped the handle with both hands, breathing hard as he rotated. "What does this do?" he asked, panting.

"We're turning this craft manually," Orion explained, his eyes on the flight monitor. "I already applied a patch from the service module, using a bot. That ought to hold us. Later, when we get to the space station, we'll repair the breach for real."

"OK." Mars stopped talking as he concentrated all his energy on turning the wheel. Orion was right. It was taking everything to hold on so that Mars wouldn't find himself thrown against the walls of the flight deck.

Meanwhile, Julia and Orion continued steering while Mars kept turning the wheel and announcements blared overhead: low pressurization, acceleration, deceleration, oxygen levels, radiation levels. Then a few minutes later, the announcements stopped. The lights came on in the room. And the spinning stopped. Mars let go of the wheel and floated gratefully to an open chair. Through the monitors, he could see the spacecraft moving forward as Orion finished entering coordinates into the panel.

"Back on autopilot," Orion said. "And on track to reaching Pruitt Space Station at expected arrival time."

"Excellent work, Orion," Julia said. "Of course, you *are* the best pilot at Pruitt Prep."

"Yeah, but you're the one who spotted the breach." Orion stretched back in his chair. "So that just leaves you, Butterfly. Why are you here, again?"

"Why do you keep calling me that?" Mars asked.

"'Cause you look like one, flying around like somebody's gonna eat you."

"No, I don't!" Mars jumped up from his chair so suddenly

that the momentum spun him forward into the monitors. He leaned back, rubbing his sore arm.

"Butterfly!"

"Quit calling me that!"

"Oh, bloody stop, both of you," Julia said. She had clearly had enough. "Orion, you know who he is. He's Mars Patel."

Orion gave a good-natured smile and held his hands up in the universal gesture of backing off. Even though he looked a few years older, it was clear he respected what Julia had to say. "'Course. I was just messing with him."

"Just because this is your second trip to Mars," Julia said, "doesn't mean you get to ruffle everyone's feathers."

"I got you," Orion said.

Behind Julia, Mars noticed something strange with one of the monitors. "Hey, why is it dark in the cargo hold? Is everything OK? Did something break when we were spinning?"

Orion's smile faded. "Nope. It's dark for a reason, Butterfly. Stay out."

"Why?" Mars asked. "Maybe you should check—"

Orion stood up quickly, his feet catapulting him off the ground. "I said, stay out!"

"It's some special delivery Mr. Pruitt put Orion in charge of," Julia said to Mars. "Even *I* don't know what it is. But boy, does Orion get his shorts bunched up over it."

"Why does everything have to be so secretive around here?" Mars grumbled.

"Listen, Butterfly Breath," Orion said. "This ain't no H. G. Wells Middle School. Yeah, Julia and me know all about you and your friends back home. If you guys don't like something, you just break the rules and go to detention. Well, that's not how it works here. You mess up, you DIE."

"I think I can take care of myself," Mars said hotly. He decided to ignore the fact that just a few minutes ago he had been clutching a barf bag.

"Mars, Orion is right," Julia said gravely. "This *is* a dangerous place. Remember what just happened."

"You mean the breach?" Mars said. "I thought that was an accident and we fixed it."

Julia and Orion glanced at each other. A whole unspoken conversation seemed to flow between them.

"That breach was no accident," Orion said ominously. "That was *sabotage*."

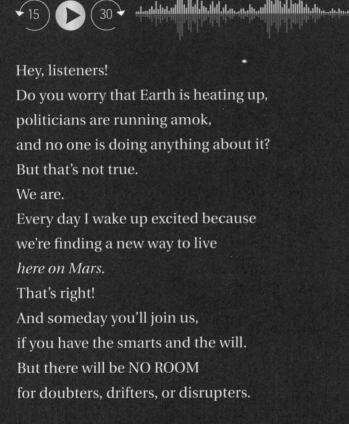

Hey, listeners!

Do you worry that Earth is heating up,

politicians are running amok,

and no one is doing anything about it?

But that's not true.

We are.

Every day I wake up excited because

we're finding a new way to live

here on Mars.

That's right!

And someday you'll join us,

if you have the smarts and the will.

But there will be NO ROOM

for doubters, drifters, or disrupters.

To the stars!

2100 Comments ⌃

staryoda   25 min ago

OP is on mars?????

allie_j   24 min ago
OMG!!!

neptunebaby   23 min ago
OMG!!!

galaxygenius   21 min ago
I knew it

staryoda   20 min ago
Take me now earth sucks

oreocookies   5 min ago
what's the catch

2
INTERFERENCE

Six Months Later

Life had fallen into a routine on board the *Pruitt 3*. Every morning, Mars did pilot training with Orion, followed by computerized lessons on spacecrafts with Julia. Then Mars and Orion hit the stationary bike, treadmill, and weights machine on the flight deck for their daily hour of exercise. For some reason, Julia never joined them. She said she had her own exercise routine, which she insisted on doing at five in the morning. Mars asked her why she couldn't do it at the same time as they did.

"I can't be hanging out every second with you guys," she said as she surveyed a flight screen. "Somebody's got to make sure we're on track."

Mars stared out the observation window at distant stars punctuating the silent and vast spacescape. The voyage was so smooth, it would be hard to tell they were moving if it weren't for the window. "Um, don't you need to take breaks, too?" he asked.

"Whizzing meteors and flying debris don't take a break, do they?" Julia said pointedly. "We have to watch out for threats to the spaceship at ALL TIMES."

Meteors and flying debris? Really? So far, they hadn't seen anything out of the ordinary in the six months since the breach. And *that* was something Julia and Orion wouldn't talk about. Why didn't they trust him? What were they keeping secret from Mars?

Orion tried to shrug it off. "It's Julia's first mission, and she wants to get it right. So give her some space. Get it? Ha, ha."

Orion had been on the last flight to Mars, so he knew all the drills and he was more laid-back. But he was not exactly an open book. The other big mystery aside from the breach was the cargo hold and why Mars had to stay away. But the more he pestered Orion for details, the more determined Orion seemed not to tell Mars a darn thing. At one point, Mars tried the cargo hold door when no one was looking, but it was locked—only Orion knew the access code. More secrets.

Still, a friendship had formed among the three of them. They ate lunch and dinner together in the crew cabin, making their way through reconstituted packets of tandoori chicken, fettuccine alfredo, and pad thai. They talked about Oliver Pruitt and the Colony on Mars, and about the mission and why they were there.

For Julia, it was a chance to do something new.

"First I was looking for the missing kids," Julia said, referring to the hundreds of children who had gone missing around the world, who were actually at Pruitt Prep. "Until I found out where they were. After that, it was seriously boring being in my flat in East London. It's not like I've got a trove of kids like me to converse with. And I love my parents, but they own a hardware store. How long can I talk about lug nuts and home repair?"

"Me? I had nothing else better going on," Orion said. "This is way cooler." Mars asked him if he missed his family. "I *am* my family," was his reply.

"Well, you guys had a choice," Mars said. "I'm just sort of here." That wasn't true. He'd had a choice. And the choice had been to protect his friends. And find Aurora. But Mars didn't know then that his choice would include going on some kind of interplanetary expedition.

"Maybe butterflies just go where the wind takes them," Orion said, grinning.

That was the other thing. The teasing. But it was different here. Not like the Boof picking on Mars in middle school for being smart or weird. Here, everyone looked out for one another. Julia gave them daily schedules. Orion always checked that the machines were calibrated just right so Mars didn't get stunned or winded during pilot training. And when they went to bed, Orion made sure everyone said good night every night. Like family.

In the afternoons, the three of them conducted experiments in the service module, where they grew zucchini, potatoes, and sugar snap peas inside an incubator, and built small robots to help with housekeeping. Mars was surprised by how busy he was. The spaceship was smaller than his tiny apartment in Port Elizabeth, but it had everything you could want, from food to rocket fuel to exercise equipment to space toilets. Still, when Mars remembered his home, he would catch his breath. How was his mom? How would she manage without him? He still could hear her voice over the phone when he'd said goodbye to her from Pruitt Prep back on Earth.

"I always knew you have a great destiny," she had told him, her voice cracking. Did she know what his destiny really was? To fly to Mars? He'd left her behind, and all his friends: Caddie, Toothpick, JP, Jonas. Were they happier without him, or had he managed to destroy their lives, too? All those weeks of detention, the suspensions from school, and not to mention being social delinquents—that was all his fault, too.

The only thing that gave Mars hope was finding Aurora. At least his other friends were safe at home with their families. But who was looking out for her? Her dad was never around, and neither was her mom. What if Aurora had gone on this mission with Oliver Pruitt because she was desperate? Because she didn't have a choice? Or what if Oliver had taken her away for some other reason? So many secrets. Oliver Pruitt might be the most untrustworthy human being in the universe. And yet here Mars was, traveling in a rocket ship to meet him. It kind of blew his mind.

Meanwhile, there was no way to get in touch with his friends or his mom. All Mars had was an interplanetary phone that used some complicated technology that Julia had tried to explain to him, but it went in through one ear and out the other.

"IP phones only connect to the Colony," she said. "They're meant for official business and emergencies. So you can forget about texting your girlfriend, Aurora."

Why did everyone think Aurora was his girlfriend?

"I'm not texting her," he said. Even though that was exactly what he was doing.

Server: interplanetary
From: thisismars
To: aurora
Timestamp: 0600

Aurora it's pretty wild in space. did i tell u I have 2 crewmates. Julia is super smart. Like Toothpick x 100.

16

Orion is a rly good pilot. They prob think I'm a dork.
Write back!!

So far, Aurora hadn't written. But maybe one of these days she would. He had to keep trying so she would know he hadn't forgotten her.

Today he texted her because it was important—the most important news of all.

Aurora—landing on Mars in 24 hours!!
See u soon I hope!

Just then, Julia's dinner tray clattered on the table as she Velcroed it down and strapped herself into a chair across from Mars. Next to the tray, she also Velcroed down a training manual labeled *Coding for the Next Century*. It was written in Russian (Julia told him when he asked). Mars's friend Toothpick had been the smartest person he'd ever known, but Julia was smarter. She knew at least three programming languages, as well French, Russian, and Japanese, and a smattering of Hindi. She only needed to hear something once to remember it, whether it was long, complicated instructions on how to deice the auxiliary chamber, or how to play backgammon.

The only thing Julia wasn't good at was patience. She floated everywhere, even across the room, in a hurry. And she absolutely wouldn't allow anyone to do anything for her. When she had trouble removing a harness strap and Mars tried to help, she said in her slow but careful voice, "Thanks, but I'm perfectly capable of unbuckling myself, Mars. Stand back!" She said the same thing when she had to trim her own hair and couldn't see the back of her head. *Stand back!* Or shutting the hatch to lower deck: *Stand back!* Mars learned that with Julia, it was always *stand back* because she could do everything by herself, thank you very much.

"Bloody boo-hoo, Mars," she said to him with her characteristic drawl, observing him now on his phone. "All you can think about is texting Aurora. Or Caddie or Toothpick or one of your other oddly named friends."

Mars shoved the IP phone into a pocket. "You texted a lot, too. Weren't you always sending me texts when we were back on Earth, warning me about Oliver Pruitt?"

"I was," Julia said, peeling back the plastic seal on a box of rehydrated mac and cheese. "But that was before I understood the mission."

"Yeah," Mars said. Mars stirred his mystery casserole. He wasn't sure what was in it because the ingredients were written in a foreign language. Was that roasted carrots? And potato? "Um, what exactly is the mission again?"

Julia's spoon stopped midway to her mouth so abruptly that a few pieces of macaroni floated away in the weightless air and she had to lean forward to catch them. "To start over as human beings! To do it better than the idiot adults back on Earth!" She cleared her throat. "Sorry, I thought it was obvious. Also, doesn't it boggle your mind that we've been traveling all these months and now we're finally about to land on Mars where we get to live in a brand-new colony built by kids like us? How many people get to do *that*? Especially me, I'd never think that with my . . . well, I never thought it would happen to me."

"Me too," he agreed. "And I finally get to see Aur—I mean Mars," he said quickly when Julia raised an eyebrow.

"Still talking about Aurora, Butterfly?"

Orion had floated into the crew cabin in his pj's. If Julia was the example of organization and attention to detail, Orion was the exact opposite, preferring to chill when he could, which was often. If he weren't an epic pilot, Julia would have strangled him already.

"Are you ever going to stop calling me that stupid nickname?" Mars said.

"No, Butterfly," he said, rummaging through the food compartment until he pulled out a gray package. "Yum, bibimbap!"

Julia looked up. "You have to heat that one extra. And stir well or you'll have lumps."

Just then a pinging sound echoed across the room.

"Uh-oh," Orion said. "We know what that means."

There was a flash of light, and Oliver Pruitt's hologram materialized in front of them. Today he was wearing his customary white space suit, and he had a five o'clock shadow on his chin as well as visible circles under his eyes. Could it be that Oliver Pruitt was actually tired?

"Greetings, my cosmic friends!" he called out. "I have been burning the midnight oil in anticipation of your arrival!"

"Us, too, Mr. Pruitt," Julia said. "We have been doing all the necessary preparations. We know that docking a spacecraft at seventeen thousand miles an hour is no sneezing matter."

Orion rolled his eyes at Mars, who grinned back. Julia was always so precise.

"Geez, don't worry. I got it," Orion said easily. "Tomorrow by this time, you'll be strolling on the Red Planet, catching some fine views of those two moons."

"Er, right," Oliver said. "Actually, we're expecting you at eighteen hundred hours."

"Say what?" Orion asked, surprised. "That's in, like, an hour!"

"That's also, sir, twenty hours ahead of schedule," Julia said. "Are you certain?"

"We're docking already?" Mars looked from one face to another.

"Affirmative," Oliver said. "That's because I increased

your spacecraft speed remotely. We have been experiencing 'interference.' Better you arrive before anyone else knows."

"Is it the Martians?" Orion asked. "Are they giving you trouble?"

Oliver's smile was steady. "Yes, but we don't let setbacks slow down progress."

"Martians?" Mars asked. "You mean like slimy green aliens with red eyes?"

"No, Butterfly," Orion said. "Mr. Pruitt's talking about a small group of Colonists giving him grief."

"They call themselves the Martians, and they're a royal pain," Julia said. "Who do you think sabotaged us six months ago when you first came on board?" She stopped as if she had said too much.

"*That's* what the breach was?" Mars asked. "Why didn't you tell me about the Martians? I mean, Colonists. What's so secret about them?"

"*Some* of the Colonists," Oliver corrected. "But listen, that's not important. I'm here to tell you to secure the spacecraft, get into position, and prepare for your arrival at Pruitt Station. You will be docking in the main area, then transferring to an Oliver Shuttle."

"An Oliver Shuttle?" Mars repeated. It sounded like one of those rides at Six Flags.

"That's right. Just a short ride, and you'll be on Mars."

"Mars on Mars," Orion said, grinning.

Oliver Pruitt's hologram shimmered. "We're all very excited!"

"Roger that," Julia said. "We're excited, too, sir! We will be ready."

"Oh, and one last thing, friends," Oliver said. "Keep this information about your arrival to yourselves. We don't want any trouble. Understand?"

"You can count on us," Orion said. "What about that special delivery in the cargo hold?"

Oliver's eyes flicked momentarily to Mars. "Continue as planned, Orion. And remember, no one is allowed in cargo hold." This time his eyes rested plainly on Mars.

Mars stared back, feeling rankled. There it was again, secrets. After all that had happened, why was no one being straight with him? What was so important in the cargo hold?

Oliver Pruitt gave a swift salute. "To the stars!"

"To the stars!" Julia and Orion said at the same time.

"Yeah, right," Mars muttered.

There was another ping, and Oliver's hologram shut off.

"OK, guys, level with me," Mars said to Orion and Julia. "Why do the Martians want to sabotage us? Why couldn't you tell me before?"

Julia looked uncomfortable. "Sorry, Mars. Mr. Pruitt likes to do things his way. He says to tell you things on a need-to-know basis. Right now, we *need* to get ready. That means you, Mars. You're always the slowpoke."

"Yeah," Orion said. "We don't need you slowing us down with your butterfly moves."

"I heard Julia already," Mars said. "Way to be an echo, Orion."

By now, Julia had dumped her food containers in the receptacle and was exiting the cabin. "Time to put on your launch and entry suits. And don't forget your helmets. I expect to see you both in the flight deck in exactly forty-five minutes."

Orion snickered. "Time to get into my fancy threads. See you soon, Fly. Don't get stuck in the door!"

"You're hilarious," Mars said, watching them go. In spite of himself, he felt a rush. After all that had happened, after all the awful things Oliver Pruitt had done to him— humiliating him in front of his entire school, kidnapping his friends, and oh yeah, forcing him to ditch everyone on Earth for this mission—Mars was still excited. He had been training for months with Julia and Orion. It had taken him weeks to figure out how to lock on the helmet and gloves of his space suit, but now he could do it quickly. (He was hardly a "slowpoke.") Mostly, he couldn't believe he would be landing at the space station and heading off from there to Mars, where he would meet Oliver Pruitt (a jerk, yes, but at least a famous jerk) and finally find Aurora.

As Mars was throwing away his food items, he heard an unfamiliar buzz in his pocket. It was coming from his IP phone. He pulled it out quickly. Was it Aurora finally? So far she had never answered any of his texts. Mars's pulse quickened as he clicked the envelope icon on the screen. But it was not from Aurora. It was from someone he didn't know. With a warning.

Server: interplanetary
From: anonymous
To: thisismars
Timestamp: 1742 hours

Mars we know all abt ur arrival. Ur in big danger.

We'll find u so don't bother hiding.

DON'T TELL ANYONE YOU GOT THIS MSG or it's

bye bye julia & orion.

3

BREAKING THE RULES

As Mars put on his space suit and grabbed his helmet, his mind went over the message. It sounded threatening but kind of dorky, too, especially that last part—*bye bye julia & orion*. Did anyone actually say that? Or was it a joke? He stopped suddenly. What if it was the Martians? Should he tell Julia and Orion, or keep quiet like the message said?

He really missed Caddie. He missed talking stuff out with her. She was a good listener, but she also cared what happened to him. When he got locked out of his apartment once in Port Elizabeth, she was the one who'd waited with him on the front steps of the apartment building until his mom came home three hours later. She was the one who had found him at Pruitt Prep when he'd disappeared from the dance that night. And when it had come time for this journey, she'd warned him not to go. He didn't listen then because he didn't have a choice. But he had a choice now, didn't he?

If Caddie were here, she'd say, *Trust your instinct, Mars.* She was big on instinct. And right now, Mars's instinct told him that he was being kept in the dark—by Oliver Pruitt, Julia, and Orion. About what was being guarded in cargo hold. What if the message on his IP phone and the secret in cargo hold were somehow related? The moment Mars made this connection, he couldn't drop it. He had to find out now. It might be the last chance he had before they docked.

The cargo hold was right below the crew cabin, so Mars got there in seconds. The only problem was that the entry was still locked with an access code. Maybe one of the other codes Mars had learned recently would work, like the one to the incubators or to the oxygen tank storage?

As Mars leaned over the keypad, he felt a hand grab him by back of his space suit.

"I knew it!" Orion's voice jabbed at him from behind.

"Let go of me," Mars said, struggling to break free. "I have to know what's in here, or—"

"Or what?" Orion leaned over him. He was wearing an orange-and-yellow space suit, his helmet dangling from his other hand. "We gotta dock at Pruitt Station in a few minutes, and I can't have you flying around out here, getting a concussion. Come now and get strapped in the cockpit. That's an order."

"But Orion, what is Oliver Pruitt hiding that—"

"You don't get it, do you?" Orion glared at him. "It's dangerous out here in deep space with dangerous people who want to destroy you."

"I know that, Orion!" Mars said, glaring back. "Like just a few minutes ago, I got this—"

"I think you DON'T know," Orion interrupted. "'Cause I already told you what happens when you break the rules."

"Yeah, well maybe I got here because I know when to break them," Mars muttered.

"Gu-y-y-ys . . . we haven't got all day." Julia's voice rang out through the intercom.

Orion pulled on Mars's arm as they climbed up a ladder to the flight deck. "You should be thankful I'm keeping you out of trouble."

Mars was fuming. Back home, his friends had looked up to him. They'd *respected* him. Here? Nothing. Maybe it was better to keep the IP phone message to himself. He didn't need Orion or Julia always telling him what to do.

Orion glanced at him. "Don't worry, Fly. It will all balance out. You'll see."

"Whatever," Mars said.

"There you both are," Julia said as they entered the cockpit. "Honestly, you guys took *forever*. Places, everyone."

"Landing sequence will activate in three minutes," came an announcement overhead. "Please turn off all interstellar devices and arrange your seats in an upright position. The door to the cockpit will autolock for your safety in two minutes."

The three of them got into their chairs and strapped their harnesses.

"Are you ready?" Orion asked.

"Systems check," Julia said.

Mars slid on his helmet and locked it into place. "Ready," he said.

Julia and Orion slid on their helmets, too.

"All systems go," Julia said. "I'll adjust the throttle when you say so."

"Roger," Orion said. "Are we ready for an adventure of a lifetime?" He grinned at Mars. "You good, Butterfly?"

"When we land," Mars said, "you're so getting a nickname, too. Like Butt Brain."

"Ha, ha," Orion said. "I'll take Superhero."

Behind them they heard the metallic click of the doors locking.

"Landing sequence will activate in sixty seconds," came the announcement.

Orion flipped the thrust switches.

"Godspeed, Orion," Julia said.

"Thanks, Julia," Orion said. "And yo, Mars. I've been hard on you, but you're still gold. You too, Julia."

"Feeling is mutual," Julia said graciously. "I couldn't ask for a better team."

"Good luck, guys," Mars said, suddenly feeling like a loser. Now that everyone was being nice, he wondered if he should have told them about the message. About what awful thing might await them at the space station when they landed? He had let his feelings get in the way. And that could jeopardize their whole arrival. Why hadn't he thought more carefully?

The lights in the cockpit dimmed.

"Landing sequence is activated," came the final announcement. "Prepare for arrival."

If only there was more time to warn them, Mars thought before he felt the spacecraft lunge full-speed ahead.

4

ARRIVAL

Julia was getting goose bumps.

Through the flight window, she could see the outline of Pruitt Space Station come into view, floating silently like an iceberg in the dark sea of space. Soon she would be on the Red Planet. Soon she would know things about it that people on Earth would never dream of knowing. And sure, she would have to use a chair again—the last six months of zero gravity had been glorious, floating wherever she needed. But that didn't mean she wouldn't be fine on Mars. She would be more than fine. She had been waiting for a moment like this her entire life.

"Throttle, Julia," Orion said.

"Roger," Julia replied, applying the switch and adjusting the speed.

Pruitt Space Station grew larger and larger as they approached. Like the International Space Station, the

Pruitt Space Station was a center for laboratory research, but it also served as an orbiting hub for Mars, where spaceships could dock and refuel, and astronauts could continue their space journey to the Red Planet. But in other ways, the Pruitt Space Station was nothing like ISS, which Julia had studied in detail online. Instead, the Pruitt Space Station was sleek and beautiful, shaped like a bullet gently revolving on its axis. From there it was a short shuttle ride to Mars, and someday, to other destinations beyond. In fact, Pruitt Space Station might very well be the future hub of *all* space travel.

Ah—more goose bumps!

"Almost there," she breathed. As they got closer, she furrowed her eyebrows in concentration. It was important to dock *Pruitt 3* carefully. She had been training hard with Orion, and she knew that even a few inches off could spell disaster.

"Easy does it," Orion said. "Mars, bring up the view of the docking platform."

"Roger," Mars said, his voice strangely flat with that one word.

Julia glanced at him. He sounded different. Maybe it was nerves. Or thinking about his Aurora friend who, frankly, Julia was sick of hearing about. From what she gathered, Aurora sounded like a nightmare, hustling off to Mars without a backward glance. Mars's other friends sounded a bit daffy too, but they clearly cared about him. She knew because one of her early jobs at Pruitt Prep was to monitor them through the drone surveillance system that Oliver had assigned to her.

That seemed like ages ago. When she had first arrived at Pruitt Prep, she was sure Oliver Pruitt was a deranged man abducting unsuspecting children. For months she had been collecting evidence from her apartment in London. She had scoured online news sites every day, and each time a kid went missing somewhere in the world, she recorded it in her database and flooded the Internet with messages, only to see them mysteriously vanish, as if someone were two steps ahead of her, canceling all her efforts. That's because someone was—and it was Oliver Pruitt!

When she had received an invitation to join his school, Pruitt Prep—no GIFT test required!—she had jumped at the chance to expose Oliver Pruitt once and for all. But when she got there, she realized the startling truth: kids weren't being kidnapped. They were being secretly *trained*. They were preparing for Oliver Pruitt's bold mission: to build a colony driven by kid ideas and kid power to form a perfect society of intellect, innovation, and responsibility. On Mars.

Some of the kids were already there. Soon she would be joining them and making history.

Julia returned her focus to the Pruitt Space Station. She

made a final adjustment as she held her breath. Closer and closer.

"Man," Orion said. "Will you look at that sucker? That's one mother of a space station. Ease up, Julia."

"Easing throttle," Julia said.

"Docking imminent," came the announcement.

"Coordinates entered," Orion said. "Prepare for docking."

Then at last, there came the sound of contact, and a tremendous *BOOM!*

They were surrounded by lights.

"Contact confirmed," came the announcement. "Docking confirmed and successful. *Pruitt 3* has pulled into port at eighteen hundred hours."

Julia and Orion cheered while Mars grinned, but it was still there. A cloud filming his face. Julia studied him. She had been with Mars every day for the last six months, so she knew when something was wrong. But there was no time to coax it out of him. She'd have to do it later. Right now, they had an Oliver Shuttle to catch.

∩

If the *Pruitt 3* felt like a tiny apartment hurtling through space, then Pruitt Space Station felt like the Ritz-Carlton, a snazzy spacious affair with gleaming walls, long corridors, and high ceilings, with windows outfitted on all sides to give a dizzying view of the universe.

"Can I stay here forever?" Orion asked as they floated along. He pulled off his helmet, and seeing him, the other two did the same.

"I thought you've done this before," Julia said.

"Sure, but did you take a look at this place?" Orion said. "It gets me every time."

Meanwhile Mars was glancing around nervously, wondering if someone was waiting in the wings to accost them. What if that silly message on his phone was actually serious? If it was the Martians threatening him, it didn't matter that they sounded babyish. All they needed was a desire for revenge and some interstellar weaponry to attack. Mars desperately hoped they would get onto the Oliver Shuttle without a hitch. At least once they arrived on Mars, they would have Oliver Pruitt for backup.

After they had exited the spacecraft, they found a robot waiting for them in the disembarkation area.

"Greetings," it said politely, hovering slightly above the ground. "Welcome to Pruitt Station! I am HELGA, your transit assistant. You may use 'she' when referring to me. I will be escorting you to the Oliver Shuttle, which will take you to Mars. Please come with me. Use the guardrails to move yourself through the corridor as needed. This is a no-gravity space station as you know."

"Thanks. Lead the way, please," Julia said as they floated

behind HELGA down a metallic corridor, pulling themselves using the guardrails as instructed. "Er, are you OK, Mars?"

He gave her quick, nervous look. "Yeah, why?"

Julia shrugged. "No reason."

Had Julia guessed about the message? But she couldn't. No one could. Not even Orion, who seemed to have an uncanny way of knowing when Mars was up to something. He glanced at Orion, who was carrying his helmet under his arm somberly, lost in thought. Mars wondered what he was thinking about. So far, Orion hadn't really talked about his life. Julia once explained that Orion was an orphan. No parents. No siblings. He'd grown up in foster care with no one waiting for him if he ever went back to Earth. This was his second trip to Mars—he had accompanied Oliver Pruitt one other time before. Once Mars had asked him to describe what it was like to be on Mars, but Orion just shrugged and said, "Why spoil it for you? You gotta be patient, Butterfly! See for yourself!" That was Orion. Always holding back. Always keeping secrets.

Then again, Mars had a secret now, too. His eyes darted around. So far, nothing bad had happened. He just hoped it would stay that way.

A few minutes later, HELGA brought them to the shuttle loading station.

"That was quick," Mars said. "And we didn't even run into anyone." Shoot. Why did he have to say that?

"I'm sorry, I am not able to interpret that remark," HELGA said. "But if you wish to initiate a running exercise program on Mars, please make inquiries at check-in."

"Not that kind of run," Mars said uneasily. He should really keep his mouth shut.

"Ha, ha," Orion said. "Mars running on Mars!"

Behind them, a silver vehicle slid along the tracks and came to a stop.

"Your transport has arrived," HELGA announced. "Please mind the gap while floating into the shuttle."

Julia and Mars entered and saw seats lined along the sides, resembling a subway car.

"All right, kiddos," Orion said from the platform. "Here's where I say goodbye. Happy landing on Mars."

Mars's head jerked up. "Wait, you're not coming with us?"

Orion shook his head. "Nah. I gotta deliver cargo to Mr. Pruitt."

The special delivery Mars wasn't supposed to know about. "You mean Oliver Pruitt is here at the space station?" he asked, surprised. "I thought he was on Mars. Didn't he say that?"

Orion shrugged. "He goes back and forth. I'm sure he'll head over soon."

Mars sighed. When would people start being straight with him?

Meanwhile, Julia had already strapped into a seat.

"Come on, Mars," she said. "Don't worry. We'll see Orion soon enough. And Mr. Pruitt, too. He's the one who keeps saying he can't wait to see us."

"Please be sure to activate the oxygen tank located above your seat," HELGA instructed. "Your helmet should engage as soon as you sit down, after which you will experience a steady flow of oxygenated air. The shuttle is pressurized, but we recommend you keep your helmets on for the duration of the short flight."

Both Mars and Julia put on their helmets and Mars sat down in his seat.

"Are you ready for an adventure of a lifetime?" Orion called out, grinning.

"Are you ready to be called Butt Brain?" Mars called back.

"Have a safe trip to Mars. To the stars!" HELGA gave a robotic smile, which was basically her metallic mouth moving into the shape of a U. The hatch closed.

As the Oliver Shuttle slid out of the tracks, there was a pinging sound.

"Him again," Mars said.

But this time there was no hologram of Oliver Pruitt,

only his voice coming through the speakers. "Welcome to the Oliver Shuttle, your one-stop transportation to the Mars Colony, where the future is built, one idea at a time! Sit back, buckle up, and prepare to be amazed!"

"If Orion's not coming with us," Mars said, "then who's piloting the shuttle?"

"No one," Julia said from inside her helmet. "It's automated. Someone at the Colony has programmed us to leave and arrive at the welcome center. Easy peasy."

"You're OK with that?" Mars asked doubtfully. "You're not worried something might go wrong?"

Julia snorted. "Human error is always worse, Mars. I trust computers more."

Oliver's voice continued, describing the fifteen-minute journey to the Red Planet as the shuttle flew out of Pruitt Station and shot effortlessly into space.

"The Mars Colony, located to the north of Monument Crater, is a thriving hub of activity, with a total of four hundred twenty Colonists living and working there."

"Whoa, that's a lot," Mars said, surprised. He tried to picture the kids already there. Was Aurora one of them? How had they all managed to travel to Mars without anyone knowing? His fingers were itching to text Aurora, but he was sitting right in front of Julia's watchful eyes, and she would complain about all his "nonofficial" IP phone use and tell him to "be responsible, Butterfly."

They were gaining speed, but the ride was surprisingly smooth, without even a tiny bump to remind them that they were in a space vehicle. Mars could hardly believe they were moving.

"As you arrive at the welcome center, be sure to sign up for Daisy Zheng's colony tour. Visit the weather tower, the greenhouse, and security wing. See for yourself what progress looks like when it's engineered by kid power."

Mars was starting to feel drowsy in the warm, cozy shuttle. Would it be so bad to close his eyes? What could happen in the next few minutes?

Around him the lights started to flicker.

"What's going on?" he asked.

"I'm not sure," Julia said. She removed her seat belt as Oliver Pruitt's recording continued overhead. "Let me take a look at the control panel."

"But we're on autopilot," Mars said. "Do you think that's a good idea?"

"At the Mars Colony, we're solving climate change even before it starts!" cooed Oliver Pruitt's voice in the background.

"I'll be fine," Julia told Mars. "I know what I'm doing."

She floated to the control area and looked at the monitor. "It says we've cleared EDL."

"EDL?" Mars asked.

"Entry, descent, landing," Julia said. "We're about to

enter Mars's atmosphere. Except, wait a minute." She frowned. "Something strange is happening—"

Oliver's recording was abruptly replaced by a clicking sound, and then someone else's voice came on the speaker.

"Greetings, newbies," said the new voice.

Mars sat up, surprised. He glanced at Julia, who seemed equally dumbfounded.

"Don't get comfortable," continued the voice, "because when you arrive on Mars, you're going to discover all the lies told to you by Oliver Pruitt, the biggest liar of all. Don't expect it to be great here. Expect to die. If the atmosphere doesn't kill you, the volcano will."

"Volcano?" Mars repeated. His stomach twisted up instantly.

"Who is this?" Julia demanded. "Tell us your name. Then get lost."

"Oh, I think Mars knows," said the voice gleefully. "Maybe not our name, but what we plan to do when you get here."

"You're the Martians, aren't you?" Julia said suddenly. "Wait, Mars. You know who they are?"

"I don't, they c-can't—" Mars stammered, not knowing what to say. Then Julia fixed such a penetrating look on him, he blurted out the rest. "They sent me a message on my IP phone. I'm sorry I didn't tell you already."

"Yeah, we're the Martians." The voice turned snide. "We're here to make your life a living hell. Unless you decide to join us. The choice is yours. Meanwhile, we're disrupting your flight and rerouting this shuttle as we speak. Forget the welcome center. You're on a one-stop destination to the lava tubes."

Julia was furious. "What? I don't believe it."

"You better believe it," said the voice, laughing now. "We know how to hack the system. Maybe you've heard of Fang, our leader? We can hack into anything. You're already reprogrammed. Ha, ha!"

Fire seemed to come out of Julia's eyes. "I don't think so!" she said fiercely. "I didn't travel for six months on a tiny spaceship eating reconstituted tuna surprise, and I certainly didn't dream of being part of a mission like this my ENTIRE LIFE, to get thwarted by a bunch of Martian freaks!"

"What are you doing?" Mars said in alarm. He started to sweat inside his space suit. This was worse than he'd feared. What were the lava tubes? And what would the Martians do once they got there?

"I'm hacking the hack, that's what," Julia said, her fingers flying off the keyboard panel. "And it's *not* going to be pretty."

Mars felt like his eyes were going to pop out of his head.

He looked out the window and was stunned to see land slamming into view. "Julia, but we're almost there! I don't think there's time!"

"I'll make it work," Julia shouted. "Buckle up."

The shuttle took a sudden nosedive as stretches of red, barren ground came screaming to meet them. Mars's thoughts turned to full-blown panic: *We're going to crash, we're going to crash, we're going to crash* . . . He brought his knees up and squeezed his eyes shut as they braced for impact.

5
LANDED, MAYBE

Mars coughed, blinking in the dark, dust-filled cavity of the mangled Oliver Shuttle.

It was a miracle. How else would you describe being in a hijacked space shuttle, rerouted by an amateur hack, then crashing into Martian soil . . . and *surviving*? By now, the thin, carbon-dioxide filled atmosphere had infiltrated the broken capsule. He was grateful for his helmet and space suit. Without them, a few breaths of Martian air would have killed him.

But what about Julia?

Mars remembered then that there was a light attached to his helmet—all the helmets had them. He quickly turned his on.

There was a stirring next to him. "We bloody crashed," she muttered. "Mars, are you OK?"

Mars stood up inside the crumpled shuttle. After so many months of floating in zero gravity, it was strange to feel his feet on the ground again. "I don't know how you did it, but you did it, Julia. You landed a space shuttle on Mars. And you didn't kill us."

By now, Julia had switched on her helmet light, too, and both their lights were casting dancing shadows around them. "I aim to please. And if I ever get my hands on those Martians, they'll be sorry they ever tried disrupting me." She looked at her IP phone. "No signal either," she observed.

"Come on, let's go outside," Mars said. "Don't you want to see the planet?"

Mars on Mars, he thought. If Orion were here, he'd say that. Now it was real. In a few moments, he would open the hatch and his feet would walk on Martian soil. Strange— why wasn't Julia clambering past him, ordering him to hurry?

"Mars, there's something I have to tell you." Julia's voice sounded odd. Not her usual slow, careful drawl. But flat. Strained. Different.

"You think it's unsafe," he guessed. "But it could be unsafe staying here, too. Like, what if the shuttle explodes or something? And don't you want to go outside?" Mars's breath rose in his throat. "We made it, Julia. We're really here! Not even the Martians can change that. We've been waiting for this moment for months."

"Of course I'm thrilled. I'm not one of your bird-brained classmates. I'm not the Boof." Julia remained on the ground. "Listen, I'm going to do lots of amazing things on Mars. I know this because I've done amazing things already. I can fly a rocket ship, I can dock it at the space station, I can program, I can hack, and I can ride horses."

"Horses?" Mars asked blankly. What was Julia getting at?

"But there's one thing I can't do." She pointed down at her legs. "I can't walk."

Mars moved forward instantly. "Are you stuck? Are you hurt?"

Julia held out her hand to stop him. "No, Mars. I'm not injured." There was a pause. "I haven't been able to walk since I was eight."

Mars stared at her through his helmet, surprised. He looked at her legs splayed out in front of her on the shadowy ground. Julia stared back, except it was the same look she gave him when she was explaining interstellar combustion and he still didn't get where everything went when he used the space toilet. "I don't understand," he said. "On the spaceship, you—"

"Floated," Julia finished. "In zero gravity, you don't walk."

"Whoa," Mars said. "So were you in an accident? Is that

why you can't walk? S-sorry—" he stammered. "Is it wrong for me to ask?" The last thing he wanted to do was make her feel bad.

"Look, I'm going to explain this only once and then we don't have to talk about it anymore. And don't you dare treat me like I'm helpless. Because I'm not. I can't walk, but I can do everything you can do and a lot of things you can't."

"Sorry," Mars said again.

Julia's voice was filling out. There was even a hint of her old humor returning. "Stop saying sorry. It has nothing to do with you, believe it or not, Mars Patel."

Mars nodded. "So it wasn't an accident."

"It's called Friedreich's ataxia," she said. "FA for short. It's an inherited, degenerative disease, which means I was born with it, and it will get worse over time. It affects the nerves and muscles in my entire body. It's also a rare condition. Like winning the lottery." Here she smiled and he smiled back unsurely. She was so calm, it was hard to know how to react. "You might notice my voice sounds slow because FA affects my speech. That's why I try to say everything clearly. And you might notice that my legs . . . well, maybe you *haven't* noticed on the spaceship."

"Because in space you could float," Mars said, "and now that we're here on a planet, where there's, um, gravity . . ."

"Exactly. My legs don't work the same way. I can't

balance and coordinate on them so I need a wheelchair. I already put in a request at the Colony, but seeing as those idiot Martians got us stuck here . . ."

"Right," Mars said.

There was a pause, and it seemed like she was waiting to see what else he would say. She looked a little worried, like maybe he was going to fuss over her from now on. The look on her face was just like when they were in the shuttle and she didn't want anyone unbuckling her harness. She wanted to do things herself.

Mars thought for a moment. "So, should I go outside and see where we landed?"

Julia looked relieved. "Yes, do what you'd normally do. Nothing's changed. Anyway, you're probably dying to take a look."

"You, too," Mars said.

She shrugged good-naturedly. "You go first. You're the slowpoke."

She smiled at him again, and then everything was OK. Even the crash, because he and Julia had made it, and now they were here. On Mars.

He stepped back and reached for the hatch, and with a great heave, thrust the door open. It was dark outside, but his eyes adjusted quickly. His boots made crunching sounds as he scooted out of the shuttle. Around him loomed steep mountaintops with jutting, mile-high cliffs.

It was shadowy where they were, but up high past the edges of the cliffs, he could see light filtering above them in a bluish, reddish haze.

They had landed deep inside a valley, where the ground was rocky and cracked, spreading away from him in all directions; it was beautiful, but it was stark and frightening, too. Never before had he felt so puny. Everything he knew seemed to get stripped away: his family, his friends, his very humanness. Was this how Earth started? Or how it would end?

"Oh my god!" Was that all he could say?

"What? What?" came Julia's voice from inside. "Is it good? Is it bad? You're killing me, Mars. Tell me."

"It's . . . red," Mars said. *Duh.* Was that the best he could do? "I think we landed in a crater. There's mountains around us; we're in a valley, but there's nothing green. Just blue and red, and the sky is so big."

"Real poetic, Mars. Blue and red. I can see it now."

"There's something way over there at the top of the crater. It looks like the dome of the welcome center. That must be it—the Colony! You did great, Julia. We're not too far off. You need to come out and see. Maybe I can—" He stopped. "Wait."

At the top of one of the cliffs, a space buggy rolled up. Then another and another. As they lined up along the edge, Mars could hear the menacing roar of engines revving.

Then a figure stepped out of one of the buggies and stood there at the edge, peering down.

"Mars Patel?" The voice reverberated across the valley through a loudspeaker. "We know you're down there. You can't hide." One by one, more figures stepped out of space buggies. God, how many of them were there?

Mars ducked back into the shuttle.

"It's the Martians," he said, breathing hard. "They're coming for us."

6
CARGO BEEP

Orion had a bad feeling. It had started with seeing his friends off in the Oliver Shuttle. Sure, he'd played it cool. He'd smiled and waved to Mars when he saw the worry pool up in his eyes. Because he knew Oliver Pruitt would have his head on a platter if he didn't get that cargo onto the space station immediately. So he hung back, made nice with HELGA, whom he reprogrammed to give him the tracking coordinates for the Oliver Shuttle. His robotics course at Pruitt Prep had finally come in handy. He was able to view the shuttle's trajectory on his IP phone as the cargo got unloaded.

There were three sealed and insulated units to unload. They were a mystery. They had been a mystery for six months. *No one goes into cargo hold. No one, Orion, but you.*

Those were Pruitt's words. And Orion knew the man meant business. It was a year ago that Pruitt's henchman,

Mr. Q, had found Orion shooting baskets at the Boys & Girls Club in Tacoma. Orion didn't really care for basketball. He preferred hockey and soccer, but the basketball court was warm and dry and beat going back to the latest foster home where he was staying with all the cats (the couple LOVED cats) and the futon he had to sleep on in the hall. The roof had a leak, and the rain that came in made the place smell dank and moldy. Nothing made that smell go away. Or the cats.

At the courts, there were no cats. No leaks. Just a bunch of high school kids playing basketball pretty badly (he fit right in) or doing their algebra homework noisily over Doritos. Enter Mr. Q. He saw Orion tossing the basketball and doing everybody else's algebra when they couldn't figure out the problems. He wasn't sure why Mr. Q was there, but when he told Orion about this school on an island where you could solve even harder problems, and have all the food you wanted and a room of your own, Orion jumped at the chance. That's how he got here, one thing after another, and he never looked back. No regrets. It was all chill.

Then he got the cargo duty. *You'll be promoted,* Pruitt promised him. *Chief flight officer, that's what I'll make you. But you mess up, and you're out.*

It was hard to be so chill after that. He saw stars in his eyes. Anything to climb up the ladder when he'd been on the bottom rung for so long. Once Julia and Mars came along, though, it was weird—the last six months felt like *family*. Waking up at the same time, eating together, and saying good night. It was a feeling that made him happy but scared, too. He tried not to care too much. Because he hadn't forgotten Oliver Pruitt's promise.

The cargo made Orion curious, especially the beeps. They came at regular intervals. His job was to monitor them, to make sure they kept going, day after day. Cargo *beep beep*. Now here he was, months later at Pruitt Space Station, the cargo being unloaded by bots, and he could soon wipe his hands free of this responsibility. Then it would be promotion time.

Even so, Orion's eyes keep returning uneasily to the dot he now saw traversing the screen on his IP phone. "I should have gone with them," he muttered. When the last cargo unit was loaded onto the delivery bed, Orion saw something strange on his IP phone. The dot had jumped out of its trajectory. It was going somewhere else!

"What the . . . ?"

One of the bots sidled up to him. "Electronic sign-off required. Please provide a facial scan."

Orion hastily leaned forward to have his face read by the bot.

"Thank you. Delivery complete," trebled the bot.

Orion floated to the space station, using the guardrails to pull himself there quickly. On his phone, the dot had jumped again, moving erratically across the screen. Something had taken the Oliver Shuttle off course. He found HELGA hovering near the platform. "What's happened to my friends?" he demanded. "They're supposed to reach Mars at eighteen thirty. Now they're completely off track. What gives?"

"The Oliver Shuttle was overtaken by hostile forces," HELGA informed him cheerfully. "During the automated flight, a system breach was discovered after entry, allowing intruders to access the cockpit and jam all communication lines. 'Greetings, newbies' and 'Expect to die' were some of the intercepted messaging."

"The Martians," Orion said immediately. He looked at his phone in disbelief. "The dot is moving too quickly. Oh god, it's going to crash! It's going to crash!"

"System crash," HELGA announced. "And impact."

Orion let out a wail. "No!"

HELGA went on undeterred. "Two life forms detected on the Oliver Shuttle. It appears that your friends survived the impact. There is movement in the shuttle detected as well. Hurrah."

Orion breathed a sigh of relief. Then he scowled. "That's it? Hurrah? Isn't anybody going to do anything about it?"

"The Martian rebels," HELGA said matter-of-factly. "They have been spotted at the perimeter of Monument Crater. Some more intercepted communication includes the following: 'We know you are down there.'"

"This is just great. The Martians are going to get them," Orion fumed. "Well, not if I can help it. HELGA, put me through to the Oliver Shuttle."

"No signal, I'm afraid," she said.

"Then I'll call the Colony instead." He entered the number on his IP phone. "HELGA, how long before the Martians reach the Oliver Shuttle?"

"In seven minutes, the Martian rebels will reach the bottom of Monument Crater."

"Come on, Daisy, pick up," Orion said restlessly. He knew the sun was sinking on Mars. Soon it would be night-fall, and temperatures would plummet. Not only that, the space suits they were all wearing were designed to carry two hours of oxygen. What if Mars and Julia ran out? What if they were hurt and couldn't get to safety? The Martians didn't need to worry about these things. They had Fang, a daring leader who had taught them to survive under the starkest of conditions, with barely anything to eat, no real heat source from what Orion could tell, and slap-ping together sophisticated machinery out of spare parts and repurposed equipment. Under Fang, they managed to own half a dozen space buggies and Orion didn't even know how—they had stolen maybe two from the Colony. How the heck had they built more? But that was Fang and the Martians for you. Resourceful, deadly, and totally unpredictable.

Now for some reason, the Martians were after Mars and Julia. The only thing that could stop them were the impenetrable walls of the Colony. The question was, would Mars and Julia get to the Colony before the Martians got to them?

7
DAISY TO THE RESCUE

How do you know it's the Martians?" Julia asked. "Maybe it's the welcome committee from the Colony."

"You can't hide from us, Mars," boomed the voice on the loudspeaker outside. "Surrender before you're disrupted for good."

"Um, that's no welcome committee," Mars said. "We have to get out of here."

"You'd have a better chance if you left without me. Go to the Colony and bring back help. I'll be OK. But hurry. The sun is setting, it's getting dark, and these space suits are going to run out of oxygen soon. They're not designed for walking on Mars for hours."

"Don't be ridiculous," Mars said. "I'm not leaving you."

"It's the only way. And anyway, it's you they want. They said your name."

"I said I'm not leaving you."

"Fine," Julia said huffily, though she sounded a little relieved. "Well, there's only one thing left to do," she said reluctantly. "You'll have to carry me."

Mars brightened. "You mean piggyback?"

Julia grimaced. "I hate that word. I'm *not* a pig. But yes, you'll carry me on your back."

Easier said than done. Both of their suits were impossibly bulky. Mars struggled to lift her off the ground; Julia struggled to wrap her arms around his neck. Fighting ensued.

"Oh bother!" Julia said, all disgruntled and still on the ground.

Just then a banging sound came from outside.

"It's the bloody Martians!" Julia cried.

Through the entry appeared a young person in a lighted helmet and green space suit. Green?

"Greetings, mates," she said. "I'm Daisy."

Daisy wasn't one of the "bloody Martians." She was a Colonist, and miraculously she *was* on the welcome committee. She had come for them on a space buggy large enough for both of them, herself, and a driver who came out to help lift Julia onto the back. With three people, it was a breeze. In seconds, everyone was loaded up and they roared away.

"We've got a nice battery-operated transport waiting for

you at the Colony," Daisy told Julia as they drove along. "It's small and very powerful. You can even go over rocks with it."

"We call it a rover," said the driver, whose name was Kaito. "There are two other Colonists with rovers."

"Excellent," Julia said. "It will be a rover party."

"Being at the Colony *is* a party!" Daisy said, delighted. "I'm so sorry you crashed. You missed the whole welcome ceremony we planned. I've got tablets for both of you loaded with maps and all kinds of information, plus we've scheduled a tour at 0700 hours tomorrow morning, when I'll show you everything. You'll be bowled over by our progress. You're going to absolutely love it at the Colony!"

Daisy seemed quite young. In fact, Mars discovered that she was ten years old, one of the youngest Colonists on the planet. So far, she had been promoted every week until she was now chief of communications. It was clear that Daisy knew everything when it came to running the Colony, and did so with a breezy certainty that was quintessentially her.

"How did you find us?" Mars asked. By now it was dark outside with only the headlights of the space buggy to show the way. Were the Martians after them? It was hard to tell.

"We lost your coordinates when you crashed, but your crewmate, Orion, phoned in with the location and said that Martians were about to intercept you."

"Orion!" Julia said. "Well, that explains everything. He can hack a broom closet for information. I bet he found a robot with a direct line to the Martians."

"Who *are* the Martians?" Mars asked, still studying the terrain behind them.

Daisy glanced at him. "Don't worry, we've lost them. And anyway, that's not how they work. They work by stealth and infiltration, not direct confrontation. They know we have the full force of the Colony behind us."

"But are they dangerous?" Julia asked.

"Yeah, because they're unpredictable. Right, Daisy?" added Kaito, who had been largely quiet during the drive. "Their leader, Fang, is the most unpredictable. Remember how they stole the space buggies from the garage in the first place? They basically walked right in and drove off with them! Nobody expected that kind of brilliance—"

"That's not brilliance, just dumb luck," Daisy said, grimacing. "Ugh. Let's forget about them. Especially that Fang person. I mean, what kind of name is that?"

Mars and Julia glanced at each other in the dark. They were both thinking that this Fang was definitely *not* someone to forget. Mars couldn't forget the ominous screech of the Martian space buggies. He finally asked the question on his mind. "Daisy, do you know where Aurora is?"

From next to him came a long sigh. Then Julia said, "Sorry. That was involuntary. Carry on."

"Julia, I have a right to know!"

"If you mean Aurora Gershowitz . . ." Daisy started slowly.

"Have you seen her? So she's here at school, right?" Mars jumped in.

"Not school," Daisy corrected. "Colony. We are post-school. Everyone here is too advanced to sit in a traditional classroom. Not when we've mastered all the basics and there's so much to do."

"All right, sorry—the *Colony*," Mars said impatiently. "But what about Aurora?"

Daisy looked uncomfortable. "I'm sorry, Mars, but I'm not at liberty to say. Rules are rules, and I'm a rules person. Mr. Pruitt wants to talk to you himself. Aurora is classified information."

"Classified?" Mars repeated.

Julia snorted. "That's a fancy way of saying somebody screwed up."

Mars glared at her. "She's alive, Julia. I know it."

"Goodness, Mars," Julia said quickly. "I didn't mean to imply she's *dead*."

Up ahead, a large dome suddenly came into view.

"We're here! That's the South Dome, the entrance to the Colony!" Daisy announced brightly. "Mars, don't worry. One thing I can tell you is that Mr. Pruitt is very thorough. He won't forget to have the most important conversation of your life with you. That's not the Colony way!" She glanced at the lit screen of her IP phone. "Will you look at that—you're just in time for the next recording of the podcast."

"You mean, like, *the* podcast—the one I've been hearing"—he was about to say *all of my life*, but that sounded a bit pathetic—"back home?"

"Oh, yes, that very podcast," Daisy said. "The Colony is responsible for broadcasting it to Earth and beyond!"

As they pulled into the compound, Mars wanted to feel more excited about everything, but instead, he was just growing more suspicious. He ought to know more about Aurora by now. Julia was right. *Classified* didn't sound exactly reassuring.

Was Aurora here at the Colony? Would he be seeing her soon? He tried to picture her, the purple-tipped hair and the way her eyes closed when she laughed. She always held herself tight, like a spring coil, and when she saw Mars, some of that would ease, her shoulders would drop. He knew these things about her, these little details, but to his surprise, he couldn't actually remember her face. He was seized with a small panic. How could he forget, when it had been less than a year? He remembered Caddie perfectly . . . that way her gray eyes flashed and her voice went down to a whisper when they said goodbye to each other at Pruitt Prep. She was being brave in front of him because she knew he was leaving.

Why was he thinking of Caddie? Mars tried to shift his thoughts back to Aurora—it was important to think of her instead right now.

Daisy directed Kaito to pull the space buggy inside a vacuum-sealed compartment. "Yeah, pull up there, next to the green platform. Don't scrape the side." She turned to Mars and Julia. "Sorry, parking can be so tricky."

After Kaito finished parking, they got out of the space buggy and entered the pressurized chamber one at a time. Once inside, Daisy directed everyone to remove their helmet and space suits. She took hers off first, and underneath them she was wearing a purple bodysuit that matched her purple hair cut to her chin. She was like a walking body of purple.

It took Mars longer to remove his space suit. It was harder than he'd thought, and he tripped over his feet as Kaito yanked the bottom half off. But at last Mars crawled out. It felt so good to be in just his T-shirt and sweatpants, without the thirty pounds of suit material. Julia got hers off by herself, but her movements were slow and labored as she pulled her legs out shakily, one at a time. By then, a rover had been brought to the chamber and Daisy assigned a boy to help pair Julia with the rover. This required helping Julia onto the machine and showing her how to strap into it while he set up the interface for her to use. While Mars waited on Julia, his IP phone buzzed in his pocket. The signal must be working now that he was at the Colony.

Server: interplanetary
Sender: orion-awesome
Recipients: thisismars; lostinlondon
Timestamp: 2230 hours

Dudes tell me u landed

omg u made me *$&*56 my pants

Server: interplanetary
Sender: thisismars
Recipient: orion-awesome
Timestamp: 2315 hours

Julia & I safe at the Colony.

Martians suck but stayed away

There was so much more to tell Orion, but just then another text flashed on his screen.

Server: interplanetary
Sender: anonymous
Recipient: thisismars
Timestamp: 2317 hours

We said don't get comfortable. Ur only there cuz we let u. wen u see the place tmrw in daylight u'll see wut a disaster the Colony rly is. U'll be begging to leave. That's where I come in.—FANG

What? He read through the message twice. Then he looked at Julia, who was strapped to her rover, cruising up and down the platform with a wild look of joy across her face.

"This. Is. Awesome!" she cried. "It literally moves just by me *thinking*!"

Daisy nodded vigorously. "It senses the slight movements of your body and calculates the direction. Kaito's roommate, Ashwin, designed it."

Mars returned to Fang's message. It was the wrong time to interrupt Julia. He decided to handle things on his own. Again.

Server: interplanetary
Sender: thisismars
Recipient: anonymous
Timestamp: 2320 hours

Ur not the boss of me. ps Fang is a stupid name

Maybe the only way to deal with Fang was to sound tough. He hoped his message would work and the Martians would leave him alone. But something told him that toughness wouldn't be enough to stop Fang.

FROM THE PODCAST

15 ▶ 30

Listeners, I have a little surprise.

GUESS WHO'S COMING TO MARS?

Hint: What rhymes with stars?

One of these days he'll be on this podcast

and tell you that someday

it can be *you*!

But first he needs to learn the ropes.

Ha, ha! Wait and see what I have planned for him!

To the stars!

1400 Comments ⊗

andromeda   25 min ago

Is this a joke

allie_j   24 min ago

I wanna come 2 Mars

neptunebaby   23 min ago

Can I send my sister instead she's a jerk

galaxygenius   21 min ago

Take my brother

staryoda   20 min ago
LA is flooding :(

oreocookies   15 min ago
what?!

staryoda   12 min ago
oops there goes Hollywood

allie_j   10 min ago
Wut srsly??

ur_face   8 min ago
staryoda is right, it won't stop raining #howitends

8

IT'S RAINING,
IT'S POURING

aira Patel had a special notification sound on her phone every time a new podcast loaded. She was in the middle of stocking the toothpaste aisle when the tinkling-glass sound came. Her boss hated it when she was on her phone, but she couldn't go outside to check. It had been literally raining for days. The streets of Los Angeles were filling with rain, and Hollywood was underwater as fancy, expensive cars floated away down Santa Monica Boulevard.

Here in Long Beach, it was raining just as heavily but at least she was a few miles from the shore. Five people had drowned this past week along the coast, pulled out by the tide. Everywhere on the news, all anyone talked about was the rain: record precipitation, flooding, landslides, and worst of all, people trapped inside their homes. When would the rain stop? No one had a clue.

But Saira did. She had been tracking precipitation patterns across the country for years. Not the way weather forecasters did with their storm radars and satellites, but collecting data from outer space. This was Saira's secret. This, and why she was doing it.

But when the glass-breaking sound came, Saira stopped thinking about the flooding and rain and her secret data. When a new Oliver Pruitt podcast came on, it meant she might hear about Mars.

"Where you going, Sara?" called Mr. Vinland, her boss, who was standing in the electronics aisle. Even now, after so many months of working here, he still didn't get her name right. How many times could she tell him, *My name is Saira!*

"Erm, bathroom break," Saira said. Just then, a customer came into the store dripping from head to toe.

"I need an automatic garage opener," he said, rainwater dripping from his chin. He looked strangely familiar to Saira, who continued to the bathroom. Had he come to the store before?

She ducked into the ladies' room and fished out her wireless headphones from her sock.

The podcast went on for minutes. First there was the part she called the brag section. Oliver could really brag forever: *I've done this, I've done that, someday history will thank me. Blah, blah, blah.* She could throw up, listening to him sometimes. Then finally he got to the part she was waiting for, the end when he addressed the listeners.

Listeners, I have a little surprise.

Guess who's coming to Mars?

Hint: What rhymes with stars?

∩

When Saira heard it, she nearly had a fit. *What rhymes with stars?* Was this Oliver's sick idea of a joke? Did it mean Mars was there? So far it had been six months since she'd said goodbye to him and entrusted his life to Oliver. She'd had so many misgivings, so much fear! Why couldn't Oliver be straight for once when he knew she would be listening? Why the tease? But that was Oliver Pruitt for you.

She went back to the toothpaste aisle. Stock the boxes, line them up. Next. It wasn't the worst job. It was better than being in Port Elizabeth. All that secrecy and sneaking around. Here in Long Beach she was anonymous while she continued collecting her data. But she missed Mars so much. She missed his unruly hair, his clothes lying on the floor, the scent of his hoodie, the way he wore it every single day to school until it was like a part of him. Mars being gone was like a limb missing from her body. Phantom pain, they called it, when you felt a twinge where your amputated arm had been. That's what it was. An invisible, lonely ache.

Then there was the awful news that Mars wasn't the

only one who'd disappeared. It had been in all the papers, including the *Seattle Times*. The parents of the other missing children were distraught. They had come after her, as if she would know anything, and never mind it was *her* son who was on board the spaceship.

Before Mars left, she'd thought the two of them could escape to Cleveland. Instead, Oliver had gotten to him first. Now Mars was gone, and maybe it was better that way. Some experts thought the rain was an aberration. But she knew it wasn't. Her secret project, in its final stages, told her so. Mars, with its toxic atmosphere, its freezing night temps, and its many volcanos, might actually be safer.

Still, she couldn't face the parents. So she had fled to California and come to this store to hide behind boxes of toothpaste. It had worked fine all these months. Just her and this job. But now the rain had started. Day after day, collecting, and along with it, her guilt.

She looked up from the rows of toothpaste and was startled to find the same man standing there, the one with the dripping chin and familiar face. Mr. Vinland was on the phone in the back, his voice carrying loudly down the aisles as it had the tendency to do because he was going deaf in one ear. He was in the middle of ordering an automatic garage opener.

"That should keep him busy," the man said to Saira, grinning.

Something about his smile made her uneasy. Where had she seen this person before?

"What do you want?" she asked.

From inside his coat he pulled out a pair of dark-rimmed glasses and put them on. Maybe he had kept them inside his coat to protect them from the rain. Or maybe he thought a bespectacled man was more threatening. "I want the data," he said.

Saira tried to pretend she didn't know what he meant. "I think you're mistaking me for someone else," she murmured, secretly frightened.

The man in the dark-rimmed glasses leaned forward. "I know who you are. You're Saira Patel. So I'll make it really clear. *I want that data.*"

Server: ad_astra
Sender: daisy_does_good_deeds
Recipients: colony_peeps
Timestamp: 0500 hours

Good morning, Colony Peeps!

It's 0500 and I thought I'd send out some early-morning reminders. Please remember to throw your food trash in the receptacles marked COMPOST. We are finding banana peels in the recycled metals bin. That's a no-no.

We are holding a special symposium at 1300 hours titled: "Mars's Moons—Why Are They So Small?" Ashwin Deshpande will be leading.

Also, we have new Colonists in room 222 and room 229. Mars Patel hails from Port Elizabeth, WA, just a stone's throw from Pruitt Prep! Julia Morrell-Cole is from South London and has already done some groundbreaking drone research for us! Let's give a warm Colony welcome to Mars and Julia! Woot woot!

On Friday, please join us for our field research trip, "Trek to Monument Crater." We have only four slots left!

To the stars!
Daisy Zheng
Colony Chief of Communication (CCC)

9
COLONY WITH MARTIANS

Mars was so tired that when Daisy showed him to his dorm room, he fell asleep immediately. The next morning, he was startled to find sunlight streaming into the small square room from a window, creating slats of light against the wall next to his bed. For one strange moment, he thought he was back home in his own bed in Port Elizabeth, and that his mother would come sailing in to tell him to pick up his clothes off the floor, and hurry up because he was late to school, and then inevitably she would stoop over to muss his hair. It gave him a sudden pang, and Mars missed his mom more than ever. He sighed, trying to push the sad thoughts away. If he thought too much about Ma, he would think this whole journey was a mistake. And he wasn't ready to give up just yet.

Mars sat up in bed, looking again at the sunlight on the

walls. That was odd, wasn't it? Sunlight that looked just like it did in his bedroom on Earth. But then he looked more carefully and he realized that the sunlight wasn't real, that the window was actually a computerized screen. In fact, all four walls were made of giant screens. He reached forward to feel the slats of light on the wall next to him. Cold. Not like sunlight at all. Near his bed on a nightstand, he noticed a tablet propped up with an audio message blinking from Daisy. He pressed the play button.

"Greetings! This is Daisy Zheng!" she chirped. *"Welcome to the Colony! Please read through the user's guide on your tablet and take the compliancy test at the end. You will then be eligible to receive your access badge and tracker. Cheers!"*

Compliancy test? Didn't that sound like . . . school? Daisy had bristled yesterday in the space buggy when he'd used that word. So why were they still taking tests here?

Mars stretched out on the bed and leafed through the user's guide on his tablet. On the first page was a map of the Colony. He spent a while looking at it, zooming in on various sections. He saw that the Colony was made up of four main tunnels, several minor tunnels, and four domes on Ground Level: North, South, West, and East. A lot of the main operations seemed to take place aboveground, but there was stuff happening underground, too. The supplies and generators were on Sublevel 1. All the dormitories were below that on Sublevel 2. Mars automatically looked at the window and remembered again it was fake. He glanced back at the map. The lowest level was Sublevel 3, which held the emergency shelter and the health ward. Cool. If he got sick, at least he knew where to go.

Mars flipped quickly through the rest of the sections—mostly rules on where to go, what to eat, and how to get things done. It all started with an access card, which he needed to get from Daisy. After a while, all the rules made his head spin.

The last section in the guide featured profiles of notable members in the Colony. There was Ashwin Deshpande, the guy who designed the rover that Julia was using. And Orion Acevedo, the lead pilot for the Colony. And Daisy Zheng, Colony Chief of Communications. Mars looked, but he couldn't find Aurora. Then again, she wasn't exactly your notable type.

Mars tried to picture the rest of his friends from Port Elizabeth living here. Toothpick would be discovering something amazing, like a new planet. JP would be building a massive new tower or walkway with their bare hands. Jonas would be hiking through Monument Crater. And Caddie . . . she would love the Colony because it would be a new way to connect to so many others. She and Mars would be talking about the place nonstop.

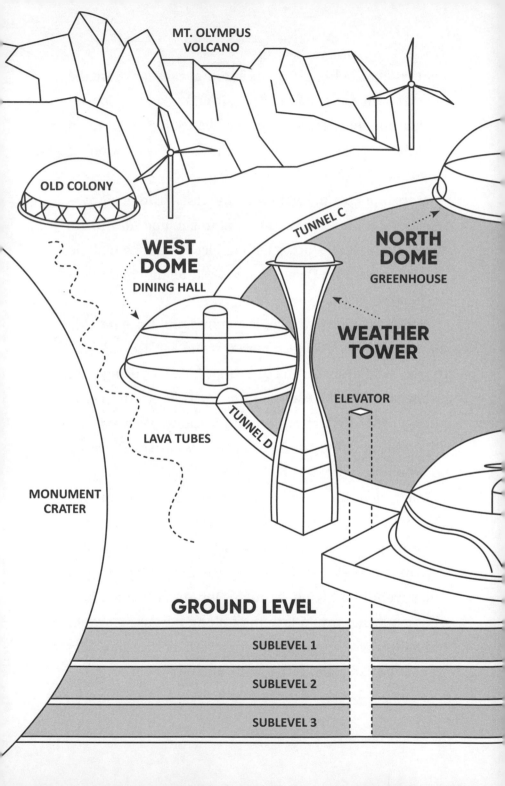

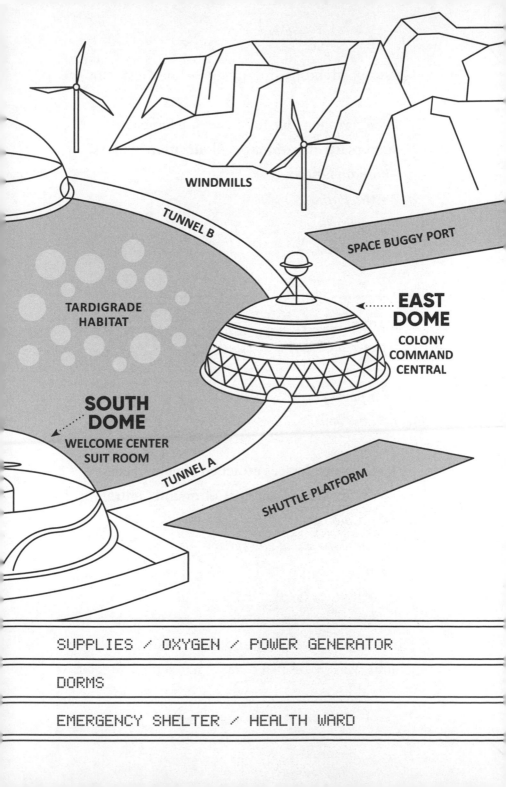

Mars skipped ahead to the multiple-choice test at the end:

1. Person responsible for achieving fame and success for his visionary colonization of Mars:

a) Abraham Lincoln

b) Amelia Earhart

c) Oliver Pruitt

d) Juju the orca

2. Access to all three sublevels of the Colony is granted to:

a) registered Colonists

b) Martians

c) your parents

d) Juju the orca

3. Trackers are devices attached to your access cards that enable Colony Command Central to:

a) track Colonists

b) evacuate in case of emergency

c) a & b

d) track Juju the orca

The questions went on and continued to be just as ridiculous. Maybe this place wasn't like school after all. As soon as Mars finished and submitted the test, there was a knock at the door.

Whoa. That was fast.

"Greetings!" Today Daisy's hair and bodysuit were completely orange. Mars had never seen anyone who literally changed their hair color every day. There were also sparkles in her lashes as she held a clipboard in her hand with a cheerfulness that Mars found unnerving.

"Your tour begins now!" Daisy announced brightly. She eyed his crumpled clothes. "Let me guess. You need an additional five to get dressed? Please hurry. The success of our colony depends on following protocol *promptly*. You might guess I like to be on top of things. Mr. Pruitt says I'm someone who 'makes time work for us, not against us'! That's my motto!"

"Uh, where's Julia?" Mars asked. He hadn't seen her since the previous evening when she was getting outfitted with the rover.

"She's already awake and visiting the weather tower."

"You mean she didn't wait for me?"

Daisy didn't say anything but continued to watch him with her sunny smile.

"OK, I'll get ready. But maybe make it ten minutes?"

"No problem!" She handed him a badge. "Wear this at all times. It's your access card. Your tracker has been activated, which means I can monitor your movements at any time. Safety first, right? We wouldn't want you to accidentally wander out of airlock and run out of air, would we? So, let's meet in the dining hall."

"Where is that?"

"Well, we're in the West Dome so it's up the elevator to Ground Level, then to your right. You should already know that from the user's guide. Maybe you read that part quickly."

Or not at all, thought Mars. "So, um, we're underground. Is that safe?"

"Being underground protects us from the deadly radiation on Mars's surface. However, the dining hall is aboveground, as are all four domes, the weather tower, and the greenhouse. You'll see. You'll see it all very soon!"

Mars nodded. "I guess that's why we have the fake sunlight in the room." He pointed to the slats of light, which he noticed in amazement had moved across the wall just like real sunlight.

"Not fake," Daisy corrected. "We don't like to use that word. The term is 'enhanced lighting' for aiding biorhythms and improving mood. At the Colony, we take mental health seriously. We have weekly check-in calls to assess your social and emotional well-being. We call it All's Well Call's Well."

"Let me guess, you came up with that?" Mars said.

Daisy beamed. "Bingo! See you in ten!"

After she left, Mars wasn't sure what "getting dressed" meant, since he didn't have anything else to wear. But when he opened his closet, he saw several outfits on hangers and folded in cubbies. He changed quickly into a pair of beige pants and a beige T-shirt. There was also a beige cotton hoodie that he pulled over his shirt. Somebody seemed to like the color beige around here.

On a table near the door, he noticed a bagel and a cream cheese packet, and a small container of orange juice. Where had those come from? Had Daisy brought them in? He scarfed the food down quickly. He didn't realize how hungry he'd been until he finished.

The elevator took a while to figure out, but finally he was able to go up with his access card. It was a high-speed elevator, like the one he'd seen at Pruitt Prep, and in a matter of seconds he reached Ground Level. As he stepped out, he saw the following sign in front of him:

WEST DOME DINING HALL
OUR FOOD IS OUT OF THIS UNIVERSE!
TODAY'S MENU:
REFRIED BEANS & LETTUCE TACOS,
IMPROBABLE "MEET" BURGERS,
STRAWBERRY SORBET SURPRISE

It didn't take Mars long to find out that all the meats in the Colony were fake (*Not fake! Locally sourced!*) and produced on-site in the Cuisine lab. Because there was no livestock yet on Mars, all food had to be grown or artificially made.

When Mars stepped out of the elevators, he was standing in the West Dome. All four domes, including the West Dome, were constructed with titanium bases and topped by a reinforced glass-dome ceiling that came down to eye level, allowing for a view of the sky and surrounding land. Mars paused to look out. It was his first view of the planet in daylight.

The ground was ochre-red and rocky, and looked like the bottom of a dried-out lake. He remembered seeing pictures of Mount Saint Helens after it had erupted in Washington State. In the photos, the ground everywhere had been covered with ash, turning the landscape barren. This place had the same dry and desolate feeling. Even the air seemed to reflect a red haze, the fine Martian dust hanging, suspended everywhere. But it was strangely beautiful, too. And calm. In the distance he could see the outlines of the North, South, and East domes, and the gleam of the steel compound surrounding the Colony.

"There you are!" Daisy exclaimed, stepping out of the dining hall. In her head-to-toe orange attire, she really did seem like another sun. "Follow me. I'll show you *everything*!"

Mars discovered that Daisy loved to talk. She loved to explain. She loved to consult her IP phone nearly every minute. After a while, Mars felt slightly nauseated listening to her, like being in the back of speeding car. But you couldn't argue that she wasn't thorough.

First they visited the weather tower, where kids were responsible for predicting wind gusts and sandstorms, and keeping an eye on Mount Olympus, the large volcano located near the Colony.

"On Earth, I lived near Mount Saint Helens," Mars said. "Mars kinda reminds me of what it looked like when it erupted. You know, like, nothing growing anywhere near there for a long time."

One of the kids sitting in front of a weather terminal smiled at Mars. "Don't worry, it's not like that here. We're on Mars. The volcanoes are totally safe!"

"Yeah!" said the boy next to her. "And we're monitoring them just in case."

"You never know," Daisy said cheerfully.

On the way out, at the base of the tower, Mars noticed a door.

"Where does that go?" he asked.

"Oh, that," Daisy said. "No one goes there. It leads to the Old Colony."

"Old Colony? What's that? I thought this was the only place on Mars."

Daisy shook her head. "No, the original colony started on the other side of Monument Crater, where you crashed. But it couldn't be expanded because of the lava tubes."

"What are lava tubes?" Mars asked, surprised. Every question seemed to lead to another question.

"They're tunnels that formed when the volcanos erupted billions of years ago and the lava flow carved them through the ground. The lava went away, but the tunnels remained. This door—it might lead to a lava tube. I'm not sure. It's always been shut. Come on, there's lots more to see!"

Next, Daisy took Mars down the elevators to the power generators and the oxygen supply room on Sublevel 1, where a machine was hooked up to convert carbon dioxide from the Martian air into breathable oxygen. Mars could hardly keep up with all he was seeing. He remembered thinking how state-of-the-art Pruitt Prep had seemed on Earth, but the Colony took it all to another level. Everything was compact and streamlined, from the tunnel walls to the high-speed elevators to the very air that was so highly regulated it was neither hot nor cold, dark nor light, and would adjust to each person's needs. Just now, the lights had brightened in the oxygen supply room as soon as Mars and Daisy entered. When they left, the motion sensors dimmed the lighting immediately. In the hallway, a wall bot that had detected Mars's hydration levels asked if he wanted a cool drink.

"Sure," Mars said, surprised.

Immediately a carton of water appeared from a side panel. Whoa. There seemed to be a solution for every problem because somebody had thought about it.

From Sublevel 1, Mars and Daisy returned to Ground Level and the South Dome, which was also the front entrance to the Colony and the entry to the shuttle platform.

"I see you're quiet," Daisy observed.

"Yeah, just speechless," Mars said. "Like, is this Mars or a movie set?"

"This is completely the real deal," she said seriously. "Not a set. We're now in the welcome center, where you would have arrived last night if you hadn't crashed." She pointed to an entryway. "Over there is the airlock to the shuttle platform. But the platform isn't pressurized, and we're not in our space suits, so we'll skip going out there for now. We had a total of three Oliver Shuttles, until you crashed one of them. Now we have only two. One of them Orion uses to go back and forth to the space station. It holds up to twelve people. The other Oliver Shuttle is the Lifeboat, which carries four people, to be used in emergencies."

"Emergencies? Like what emergencies? The Colony blows up?"

Daisy laughed. "Of course not, silly. Still, we always have to be prepared. Since the Lifeboat is designed for emergencies, it only flies on manual, so it doesn't need any interaction from the control room. Oliver Pruitt was *very particular* about that. Which is why he gave me the *extra* task of making sure that the Lifeboat is always fueled, stocked, and ready to go. This is in addition to being in charge of launching all the Oliver Shuttles and servicing them when they return to the station. Tall order, isn't it? But that's me. Even if I'm the smallest person at the Colony!" She pointed to another room. "Space suits are there. Simply show them your access card. But no need to do it now, as you won't be going outside until after you've been trained."

Daisy led Mars down Tunnel A to the security wing. She explained that this was where Colony Command Central was housed, and that access was restricted to highly trained kids, whose job was to track "nefarious activity."

"Like the Martians?" Mars asked.

Daisy gave her customary response whenever the Martians were mentioned. "Ugh," she said.

"So I can't go in?" he asked.

"Um . . ." Daisy consulted her clipboard. "Nope. Not for another week."

Just then the door to the security wing opened. To his surprise, Julia zipped out on her rover. She was wearing a similar beige T-shirt and leggings. "Mars! Finally awake, are you?"

"You're here already?" Mars asked, taken aback. "Wait—how come *you* can go in?"

"I have security clearance," Julia said. "I trained this morning. They put me on the fast track and now I'm an intelligence deputy officer. That means I know where everyone is, including you."

"I don't believe it," Mars said.

"Believe it," said a familiar voice.

Mars turned around. "Orion! You're here, too!"

Orion struck a pose, laughing easily in a beige sweatshirt and beige cargo pants. Seriously, what was up with the beige?

"Daisy summoned me by IP phone." Orion grinned. "Plus, somebody's gotta check up on you, Butterfly!"

"Hooray, the *Pruitt 3* space crew reunites!" Julia said.

"For real," Orion said. "Julia, me, and Butterfly."

"Butt Brain!" Mars returned gleefully. "I almost forgot about *your* nickname."

Julia rolled her eyes. "Surely you could be more creative, Mars."

Mars laughed. Even though it had only been a day, he

already missed the three of them hanging out. He noticed how with Julia on her rover, she was almost the same height as Orion. It was on the tip of his tongue to ask if Orion knew Julia couldn't walk. They seemed to know so much about each other already. Julia was the one who'd told Mars that Orion was an orphan. But did Orion know about Julia's past, too?

"Sorry to interrupt," Daisy said, "but I have to get back to Colony Control to upload a podcast. That's why I called Orion to finish this tour. Orion—bring Mars back when you're done."

"Yes, ma'am," Orion said.

"Have a good day, all!" Daisy flashed her signature smile, and her small, bright orange figure disappeared quickly through the door of the security wing.

"Does she run on batteries?" Mars asked. "Plus, how come she gets to wear all that color and we have to wear these ugly beige clothes?"

"I dunno, I kind of like the beige," Julia said. "Like we're putting the attention on us, not our clothes."

"Or somebody dumped a whole bag of mud on top of us," Mars said.

"It's standard protocol, yo," Orion said. "Beige is good for hiding stains, and easy to spot against the Martian surface."

Wow, they really did think of everything. "But that still doesn't explain Daisy," Mars said.

Orion snickered. "Daisy says she's a rules person, but she wants to stand out. Still, you got to hand it to her. This colony couldn't run without Daisy Zheng. She's over-the-top organized, she knows what everybody is doing and thinking, plus she knows the place like the back of her hand."

"I think Daisy is amazing and this place is amazing," Julia said. "Why would anybody want to live on Earth when they could be here?"

"Well, I kinda miss grass and trees," Mars said.

"Oh, pshaw," Julia said. "We can always *make* those. With technology, you can make anything. But you can't make stupid go away."

"Julia's right," Orion agreed. "Did you see the greenhouse yet?"

Mars shook his head.

"Come on. I'll take you there. They're growing vegetables at twice the rate they grow on Earth. That's what I call progress."

Mars nodded. "Yeah, I guess."

"We just have to keep the Martians out," Orion said.

"Are they really that bad?" Mars asked. "I mean, they didn't even come after us with their space buggies."

"They're dangerous, y'all," Orion said. "You got out because Daisy came to get you. Next time you won't be so lucky. All they need to do is crack your helmet open, and the Mars air will kill you in minutes. Watch your back, Butterfly. And don't do anything stupid."

Mars rolled his eyes. "Gee, feels like we're back on the spaceship."

Julia grinned. "Well, you *are* still the slowpoke, Mars."

There was a pinging sound.

"Oh my god, you mean he can materialize anywhere?" Mars asked. "Well, at least I get to ask him about Aurora. He can't keep her away from me forever."

"Mars."

Mars jumped. Hologram Oliver was in his white suit, but this time the reception was so good it was like he was standing right next to them.

"Sorry to startle you, Mars," he said. "That's technology in my colony for you. Where else can you virtually sneak up on a person? Ha, ha!"

"So true, sir," Julia agreed. "My mind is boggled by it all."

"Yeah, I'm digging it, like I always do, sir," Orion said.

It was strange how deferential his friends became around Oliver. What was it that made everyone kiss up to this guy? Even Mars found himself stumbling over his words.

"Mr. Pruitt, um, it's cool here and all, but I need to know: Where's Aurora? I made a promise to her. And you made a promise to me, too." Strangely, Mars felt his heart beat a little faster. Why was he getting so nervous?

"Ah yes. Promises." Oliver nodded gravely. "They seem to matter a great deal to you."

"Yeah," Mars said. "Because I don't break them." Saying that made him remember that day back home in the school parking lot when Aurora was crying because her dad had stood her up for the millionth time and Mars told her he would never do that—that he would never say he'd be there and then go back on his word.

"Well, you must know," said Oliver, "just because I promise something doesn't mean I can control what someone else does."

"What are you saying?" Mars asked, his voice rising. "Do you mean she *isn't* here?"

A silence filled the air.

Julia's rover beeped. "Low battery," it murmured.

"Sorry, I have to plug in," she apologized. She guided herself to a charging station nearby and connected her rover with a purple cable.

Meanwhile, Mars was shaking. How could he have been so stupid? "You lied to me!" he shouted.

"Dude," Orion said. "Dial it down."

"No, no. He has a right to be upset, Orion," Oliver said. "I admire your loyalty, Mars. It will serve you well in my colony. Now listen, Aurora *was* here. She took a shine to the place, and she was a natural green thumb."

"Green thumb? You mean *plants*?" Mars asked. This didn't sound like the Aurora he knew. On her apartment balcony in Port Elizabeth there had been a line of dead ferns that were never watered. Plants didn't stand a chance in the Gershowitz household.

"Absolutely, Mars. She was assigned to work on a new strain of *Brassica napus*—also known as red Russian kale. But here's what happened: the Martians broke in through the greenhouse. They seized her in the middle of a horticultural experiment."

Julia gasped. "They kidnapped her?"

Hologram Oliver seemed to waver with emotion for the first time.

"I'm so sorry," he said to Mars softly. "We tried everything. We looked for her everywhere. I'm sorry I didn't tell you before, but I didn't want to upset you, and I kept hoping that somehow we'd get Aurora back before you got here."

"Something doesn't make sense," Mars said, his voice rising. "You said she was on Mars when I was still on Earth. But that's impossible. She must have been still been traveling and—"

"Fine, so I fudged the time," Oliver Pruitt interrupted. "Aurora wasn't on Mars yet, so I created an artificial message from her using a copy of her voice. I had to do this, Mars. You needed to hear something from her or who knows what you would have done before takeoff. Like removed your harness. Or hyperventilated. It worked, didn't it? Because you came. And she *was* here until the Martians got her. And now you see why they have to be defeated."

"Those Martians are the worst," Orion said darkly. "They're a pain in humanity's behind."

Mars shook his head. "No, I'll tell you who is." He pointed to Oliver. "You! Why didn't you tell me all of this before? Why did you lie about Aurora? Why did you let me come all the way here, and let her get taken? Nobody is safe around you! Nobody!"

For the first time, Oliver looked stricken. Gone was the smugness, the arrogance. There was something else on his face. Could it actually be remorse?

"That's not true," he said. "I—" His hologram hand reached out to touch Mars's shoulder. But what good was that? Oliver Pruitt couldn't even bother to be here in the flesh. He was just a beam of light. Nothing more.

Mars stepped back angrily and ran down the tunnel.

"Mars, wait," Julia called after him. "Darn, I'm still

recharging." She stared at the unit on the wall, which read 4 PERCENT. "Orion, you have to stop him. You know he's liable to do anything, and he hasn't even been trained."

"Don't worry. I'm on him," Orion said. "Oh, and Mr. Pruitt . . ."

But Oliver Pruitt was already gone.

FROM THE PODCAST

Listeners—do you ever start with a plan
that turns into a DIFFERENT plan?
Sometimes we can't control the universe.
Sometimes the universe has
other plans for us.

But I'm a firm believer
that even when we have to make those new plans,
we still get to decide who we want to be.
We still get to be in control of ourselves,
universe or not!

To the stars!

1100 Comments ⊗

andromeda   30 min ago
I wanted to be a singer, now maybe I'll be a dentist
#planschange

allie_j   17 min ago
I want to be an astronaut . . . i still do #stickingtomyplan

neptunebaby   16 min ago

Does anyone PLAN to get flooded?? #howitends

oreocookies   15 min ago

Our house is flooded . . . i have to stay with my aunt

#planschange #howitends

staryoda   12 min ago

I got a boat! #planschange

allie_j   10 min ago

We need to go to mars #plans!!

ur_face   3 min ago

How do we know it's better there??? #howitends

10

KEEP SAFE

At first Mars wasn't sure what to do. All he could think about was Aurora being kidnapped by the Martians and Oliver Pruitt doing nothing to stop them. What kind of leader was Oliver Pruitt anyway? But then as Mars stormed down the tunnel, he started to calm down as a crazy idea formed in his head. And he thought it might just work.

The Martians had found Mars after the crash in Monument Crater. What if they could find him again? He just had to use his IP phone before he went out to the surface, and boom, the space buggies would track his location in an instant. Mars shuddered, remembering the night of the crash, when he saw those figures standing at the top of the crater, their shadowy silhouettes looming over the valley next to the revving engines. There was no telling what they were capable of. Mars just hoped Aurora was safe, but he wouldn't know unless he found her. And if he could get Fang and the Martians to kidnap him now, they might lead him to Aurora.

All Mars needed was a space suit. And *that* was easy. Mars remembered Daisy pointing out the suit room in the South Dome, which was down this same tunnel.

When he got there, Mars presented his access card. "I'd like my space suit returned to me."

A boy with cropped hair took his card. "I'll need you to sign off," he said. He gave Mars an electronic tablet to sign. "And what will be the nature of your excursion?"

"Um . . . I'm collecting samples," Mars said. "I'm growing basilica rumpus."

The boy raised an eyebrow.

"You know, Russian kale," Mars said without missing a beat. "In the greenhouse. They need special, um, Martian sediment."

The boy nodded. "Got it. Sign here. I'll grab your suit. While you're waiting, please look over this safety checklist that we give all Colonists before they make an external trip."

While the boy disappeared into another room, Mars looked over the list.

KEEP SAFE!

Are you planning an excursion to the Mars terrain? Here at the Colony, it's safety first!

Below is a list of common dangers to avoid while outside. Remember to stay suited at all times and monitor your oxygen levels! To the stars!

1. Carbon dioxide—don't breathe it!
2. Radiation—anywhere and everywhere
3. Toxic soil—yep
4. Extreme heat (daytime)
5. Extreme cold (night)
6. Sudden gale-force winds and sandstorms—watch for flying debris
7. Cracks in helmet or suit—death!
8. Exploding space buggies—don't let those engines overheat

The list went on, but Mars stopped reading because just then the boy returned with the space suit.

"It's been examined for cracks and tears," he said. "It's all good to go."

"Great," Mars said.

"To the stars," the boy said.

"Yep," Mars said as he hurried out, the safety list floating to the floor behind him.

⌒

It was easier leaving the Colony than he'd expected. The airlock from the South Dome didn't require a code, just an access card, which Mars had. After he went through, Mars found himself standing outside in the courtyard at the center of the four domes that formed a square around it. From here, the domes and their connecting tubes looked massive and intricate. The Colony was a work of art and science.

A strange pride filled Mars—Oliver Pruitt had done it, he'd colonized this planet, and the kids had designed and built everything. No matter what anyone could say about Oliver Pruitt (like that he was diabolical and deranged), he still *did* things. And he did them first. Now, because of Oliver's twisted genius, Mars was here walking on the Martian surface. You had to hand it to the guy.

Only . . . what should Mars do next? How was Fang supposed to reach him if he was stuck inside the courtyard? Maybe he should walk around and find a way out. Easier said than done.

The space suit weighed a ton. Like he was carrying a bag of bricks on top of him. And the suit was insulated and pressurized, which protected him, but made him totally hot. He could already feel himself sweating under his arms and around his neck. For a moment he considered turning around. Was this really a good idea? But then he kept going. It was time to *do something*. He'd already allowed Oliver Pruitt to get away with too much.

And yet . . . there had been something different about

Oliver this time. When he appeared in front of them, if Mars didn't know better, the man seemed a little sad. What could he be sad about? He had his Mars Colony, didn't he? And he certainly didn't care what happened to anybody living there, including Aurora.

Suddenly Mars heard a terrible roar. He froze. The sound was terrifying and yet strangely familiar. His mind reeled, trying to remember where he'd heard it before. He didn't have to wait long. Around the side of the dome, the source of the sound came at him. Mars shrank back.

It was a tardigrade. On Mars.

Part spider, part wolf, part something that had no name, Mars had seen this gigantic, hybridized creature for the first time on Earth, back at Pruitt Prep. It had been cross-bred by the school and then unleashed on whoever dared to enter the school unlawfully. But this one was even bigger, like the size of a minivan. And it was bellowing loudly, opening its large mouth at him.

As the tardigrade ran toward him, Mars grabbed the first thing he could find—a grainy rock. He pitched it hard, and the rock went soaring, landing in the tardigrade's mouth. The creature stopped abruptly. Mars watched in horror and fascination. Would it work? Would the rock actually stop the tardigrade from attacking him?

Behind him, a powerful arm dragged Mars back.

"Aaaaaaaagh!" Mars yelled.

"Quiet!" Orion's voice hissed in his ear. "Come while he's distracted."

Mars scrambled around, and together they ran. Mars looked to see if the tardigrade was behind them, but it was standing where they'd left it, its jaws like metal traps working. It was still chewing on the rock! Orion pulled Mars all the way back to the South Dome, through the airlock, until they were inside again.

Orion removed his helmet. "Are you NEVER going to learn? Those tardigrades were born and brought up here on Mars. They help us move boulders and dig. Leave it to you to piss off one of them."

"You mean that thing is trained?" Mars asked. "It sure didn't look that way."

"That there was Tartuffe. He can be an angel. Unless you startle him. Like sneaking up on him or coming out the wrong door. Hmm, let me think. Wait, you did all of those."

"How would I know?" Mars muttered. "I can't know everything about the Colony."

From his pocket, Orion pulled out a sheet of paper and held it up to Mars.

9. Tardigrades—friendly but unpredictable.
    Don't startle or they'll attack!

"I guess I missed that one," Mars mumbled.

"Leo says you forgot this safety list when you walked out of the suit room. Good thing I stopped there first and he filled me in on your stupid idea. Growing Russian kale. I didn't know butterflies were farmers."

Mars scowled, mostly because he knew Orion had a right to be mad.

"It's time you got some punishment to fit your crime," Orion said.

"I have to find Aurora," Mars said fiercely.

"I don't think so. Let's just say you're gonna get to know the tardigrades real well." Orion snickered. "But first we get you a shovel."

So the adventure continues.
Kids aren't missing, they're coming HERE.
The choice is theirs. The choice is yours.
Aurora Gershowitz has choices, too.

Still, it's important to have rules.
Because if there's a crime,
there has to be punishment.
Isn't that only fair?
Mars will find out soon enough!

To the stars!

975 Comments ⊗

andromeda   28 min ago
Who's aurora??

allie_j   25 min ago
i heard tickets 2 mars r selling out fast

neptunebaby   23 min ago
LA is a lake someone make the rain stop #stoptherain

staryoda 20 min ago
is the rain the crime or the punishment #stoptherain

oreocookies 12 min ago
whoa that's deep

neptunebaby 11 min ago
I can't even

fang_Q 9 min ago
OP is a serious pile of crap stop listening to this podcast

revolt

ur_face 8 min ago
wut? shut up already fang #stoptherain

11
EVEN THE ROMANS HAD TO POOP

The next morning, Mars found another audio message from Daisy.

"Greetings! You've been given your first assignment! Please report to the main floor at once!"

When Mars got there, Daisy was already waiting for him. Today she was sporting a neon pink bodysuit, and her hair was up in a pink bun. How did she do it? How did she change hair colors so readily? Meanwhile, Mars noticed a shovel leaning against the wall. He felt a sense of dread, remembering what Orion had said. Hadn't he talked about crime and punishment?

"Mars," she continued. "It was established that you broke Section 2.2 of the Colony Constitution—Unauthorized Excursion, as well as Section 4.8—Provoking a Tardigrade."

"Yeah, but I didn't know—"

"As a result, you are now assigned to tardigrade sanitation control."

"What's that?" Mars asked suspiciously, still eying the shovel.

"Tardigrades are darn messy," Daisy said. "They have to eat a ton to maintain their size and weight. And what goes in has to come out. In heaps. Your job is to shovel those heaps into bins."

"I'm shoveling tardigrade poop?" Mars said in disbelief.

"Think of it as environmental control," Daisy said with her same grating cheer. "Rome wasn't built in a day. Neither was the Colony. And even the Romans had to poop."

Server: ad_astra
Sender: daisy_does_good_deeds
Recipients: colony_peeps
Timestamp: 1430 hours

Good Afternoon Colony Peeps!

Reminder that this evening at 1800 hours it's "Bring Your Favorite Science Experiment to Dinner." What are YOU working on? What would you like your fellow Colonists to know about your latest research? Feel free to bring slides, handouts, computer programs, horticultural trays, or any small robotic artifacts to the dining hall for an informal Q&A. Please no radioactive or biohazard materials. Let's keep it safe!

Also, remember that the recycled metals bin is for metals only! Not old T-shirts or mismatched shoes! If you have clothes to repurpose, please speak to Greta or Toby in laundry.

To the stars!
Daisy Zheng
Colony Chief of Communication (CCC)

12

WATCH YOUR BACK

When the man in the dark-rimmed glasses showed up in the store asking for the data, Saira thought she was finished. Not only had he found her, but he knew what she had been doing. He knew she had been collecting the data; he must know about the secret project. He might even know that she had enough that she could go to the authorities.

But then Vinland came up to them in the aisle. "I can't find that model of garage opener," he told the man. "I think you'll have to try the Home Depot." Vinland grimaced. "Though with this weather, your best bet is ordering online. Home Depot is in the middle of the mudslide."

"Yeah," Saira said, relieved for once that Vinland was there. "You better be careful driving home. Who knows when this rain will end?"

"Well . . . someone does," the man said, looking at Saira.

Vinland didn't notice the insinuation. "If you do, tell me! I was supposed to drive to Baja with my wife. Some vacation that turned out to be. I bet San Diego is in the Pacific Ocean by now. I hear whole neighborhoods are gone—houses, cars, driveways, everything."

The man with the dark-rimmed glasses nodded. "It's bad in Seattle, where I'm from. Sea-Tac Airport is closed, which means I won't be able to get back today. I'll have to wait. In fact," he said, still looking at Saira, "I can be back in the store tomorrow. It gives you a day to get what I need."

"I don't think so, buddy," Mr. Vinland said. "But I don't get it—you need a garage opener in Seattle? Where exactly are you parking your car?"

The man laughed. "I have a car here, too. This is my second residence. With this rain I really need to park my car inside. And I heard this was the place to come. I'll be back tomorrow. It's not like you're going anywhere, right? Not when I can track you on my map."

Vinland shrugged. "OK, you do that. You track a stationary store on your map, bub. Ha, ha." He walked away, the conversation evidently over. Meanwhile, Saira understood the veiled threat. The guy in the dark-rimmed glasses would be back tomorrow. And he'd track her down if she disappeared. Except that he didn't know who he was dealing with.

"The door is that way," she said sweetly. "Watch your step."

"Watch your back," he said.

13
SIGNALS

Hours melted into days. Mars swore against Orion. He blamed Oliver Pruitt. But he kept shoveling. The tardigrades were prolific. They didn't seem to eat much except for reconstituted hay. But whatever they ate came out as big, round balls of excrement that had to be collected into bins to be used for fuel as well as manure for the greenhouse. Nothing on the Colony was wasted. Not even the piles of poop that were taller than himself.

"Ugh," Mars said out loud. What would his mom say if she saw him now? Or Caddie and JP and Toothpick? How would he live this down?

On his first day on the job, Mars was petrified of the tardigrades. It didn't help his nerves that he was armed with a tranquilizer dart that was stored in a compartment on his left boot. The dart would deliver a very potent sedative that would knock out a tardigrade for several hours—the only issue being that it had to be administered firmly into the skin. The only way to do that was up close, if Mars was "about to be stampeded," according his briefing guide. Great. He'd rather keep his distance.

Tartuffe was the largest tardigrade, at a whopping height of ten feet, but the others were only a smidge smaller. Emi farted a lot and would often fall asleep in front of the door, blocking it so Mars couldn't get back in. And Duke, who was the youngest, would run around the courtyard and get hyper. Gradually, as the fear of being stampeded wore off, Mars found himself getting used to these creatures. They were covered with a very fine coat of gray fur that seemed to keep the Martian dust off, though they were often seen grooming themselves. Their bodies were immense and round, and not unlike the four domes of the Colony. In spite of their size, they were remarkably agile and fast, their eight legs moving quickly over the rock terrain. But they were not really spiders, and they were not really wolves. They were unlike anything else Mars had ever seen. They would study him with their multiple eyes, sidle up surprisingly close, and grunt at him. And the rocks. They loved the rocks—the kind he had thrown at Tartuffe the first time. At first Mars wasn't sure why, then later he found out the rocks were full of salt deposits—proof that water used to exist on Mars. He learned this as he was reading about the Martian surface on his tablet one night. Who knew salt could be such a hit?

Slowly Mars got Emi not to sleep in front of the door. He got Duke to calm down. And Tartuffe, who was the smartest one, stopped bellowing at him. The salt rocks were a tasty miracle with the tardigrades, the only thing that made poop duty bearable.

Meanwhile, the Colony was humming with activity. Plans to build more domes were underway, Daisy was broadcasting podcasts at an amazing clip, and the greenhouse was flourishing with more crops (not to mention a steady flow of manure). Not only that, in the weeks since their arrival, Julia had been promoted to chief intelligence officer.

"I love my job!" Julia seemed to say at nearly every meal.

"The Colony is the best!" Daisy would say back.

And the two of them would talk about all the plans that were coming up, how everyone got along without any problems, and how the Colony was everything that Earth had never been.

"Oliver Pruitt was right," Julia said. "It *is* better here."

"For sure," Orion agreed. So far he had made half a dozen trips to the space station to deliver fresh supplies of produce from the greenhouse and cylinders refilled with oxygen generated from the power-supply room. He was also bringing back new species produced in the space station labs to plant in the Colony greenhouse. He was helping to make the Colony and the space station better.

Everyone was doing important things. Everyone was enjoying Colony life. Everyone except Mars.

"Are we ever going to see Oliver Pruitt for real?" Mars asked one day while they were having dinner. He was feeling depressed. He hated his job and he'd failed his mission. No Aurora. No way to find her. Meanwhile, his family and friends had been left behind on Earth for good.

"He has to stay at the space station," Daisy explained. Today she was wearing a neon blue bodysuit that glittered where the track lighting hit it. In her hair she had woven golden ribbons that dangled over her ears.

"I heard it's because of the Martians," said Julia.

"It isn't safe here with them crawling around like insects."

"You really don't like the Martians, do you, Daisy?" Mars asked.

"What's there to like?" Orion asked. "They caused an explosion on our ship. They're the reason the Oliver Shuttle crashed. They keep jamming my signals when I fly, and they spam my IP phone with their punk-ass messages. Your basic nightmare."

"They ever tell you where Aurora is?" Mars asked without much hope.

"No, Butterfly," Orion said. "Next time they're shooting down my ship, I'll ask."

Julia glanced at Mars but said nothing.

"Speaking of which, I gotta go," Orion said. "Heading back to the space station. I got some oxygen to deliver for the big boss."

"Me too," Daisy said, her ribbons fluttering as she stood up. "I mean, I have to sound-check the next podcast. It's a biggie!"

After Orion and Daisy left, Julia leaned over to Mars. "Let's play some chess. It's been a while since I walloped your behind."

"Au contraire," Mars said. "Since it will be me kicking yours."

They set up one of the game boards that was always left on the dining tables for kids to use. Outside the dome, the sun was setting, and dishes clattered as kids deposited their trays on their way out of the dining hall. Soon it was just Mars and Julia alone under the glow of track lighting.

"You sure have been mopey," Julia observed. "I guess you aren't a natural pooper-scooper." She moved her rook.

"Sorry, Julia, we can't *all* be chief intelligence officers," Mars said.

"We each have a job at the Colony," Julia said. "The

Colony wouldn't run if we didn't all pitch in. The tardigrades aren't so bad."

"Try standing behind them," Mars said. "You'll have a different opinion."

"Well, at least your helmet blocks out some of that, um, wind." There was a notification sound from her phone. She glanced at it in surprise. "Hmm. That's curious. Looks like they've moved."

"Who? The tardigrades? They usually sleep after the sun sets."

"No, not them." She paused to check if anyone was around, then leaned toward Mars. "Remember that day the Martians overtook our shuttle and we crashed? Since then, I've been tracing their signal. That Fang keeps them moving, but they can't go too far because they need to stay close to the Colony and steal supplies to survive."

"So where do they go?" Mars asked, interested.

"It appears they've been staying in the lava tubes. See, here's the Colony map on my phone. This is Monument Crater, where we crashed. This is Mount Olympus and the lava tubes." Mars looked where Julia was pointing at the tiny map on her screen. He actually knew it pretty well by now. Ever since he'd started poop duty with the tardigrades, he'd been studying the map in his user's guide. Sometimes the tardigrades would go running off and he'd have to coax them back with the rocks without getting lost. Now he knew which domes were which, and how to get to the space-buggy port and shuttle station without having to go through the airlocks. But he still didn't know where the lava tubes were or how to get to them.

"Daisy was telling me about Mount Olympus and the lava tubes," he said. "Like the volcano carved them out, and they're underground?"

"Right. And for Fang, it's a great way to get around. See, this is where their signal is now." Julia pointed to one of the tubes. "That's where the Martians are hiding. I'm sure of it. But I can't tell anyone yet until I have more data. It's the kind of stuff Oliver Pruitt really wants to know. He's been asking us in Intelligence to find a way to contain the Martians. They've been causing havoc. Just last week they stole all our potatoes from the greenhouse. I don't even know how they got in. But we lost about ten days' worth of produce overnight. And you know, we've got to eat, too."

Mars looked closer. This might be the break he had been looking for. "Are the lava tubes safe?"

"Probably. They're underground, away from the radiation," Julia said. She looked up in surprise as she heard a chair being pushed back. "Mars," she called out as he exited the dining hall. "Wait, where are you going? And by the way, it's checkmate!"

∩

As he took the elevator down to the dorms, Mars plotted the same coordinates into his IP phone that he had seen on Julia's. But even as he did, he was already pretty sure he knew where to find the door to the lava tubes. It was the same door near the weather tower that Daisy had told him about. If he could figure out a way to get through it, he could get to the lava tubes without ever leaving the Colony. More importantly, he could find the Martians and Aurora.

First things first. He needed a space suit, because he didn't know if the lava tubes would be pressurized. Luckily, he didn't have to go to the suit room anymore. He had a bright orange suit waiting for him in his room, and it had been cleaned by the laundry staff. That was one perk of working on sanitation control.

When he reached his room, he got into his suit quickly and took the elevator back to Ground Level. He realized that he stood out in his orange space suit. What if Daisy saw him, or tracked his movement using his access card? She'd want to know where he was going. She'd probably flag him. But luckily it was late—he didn't see anyone, not even when the elevator doors opened and he stepped out. He followed his phone GPS down to Tunnel D, making a right at the weather tower entrance. A bull's-eye on his screen matched the spot he'd been headed for. He was right. It was the same door at the base. And it was just that—a door. No airlock, no fancy access control. Just a tall, impenetrable steel door with no handle.

Maybe *this* was the way the Martians had been breaking in all this time. The question was, how did he open it?

Mars didn't have to wonder too long. There was a great rumbling sound as the door suddenly slid open in front of him. But even more surprising was how quickly Mars felt himself being grabbed.

"Hey!" Mars cried out, struggling against his assailant.

But the guy was too fast. Before Mars knew it, he was handcuffed over his suit. The guy then whooped loudly in front of a camera that Mars noticed for the first time was installed at the top of the door. Behind the guy was a long, cavernous tunnel.

"Hey, Colony Control, if you can hear us," the guy said, "this is an abduction. This is when we take Mars Patel." Then he yanked Mars through the steel door and slid it shut.

Mars's thoughts reeled. If only there were a way to stop himself from getting dragged along, but Mars wasn't strong like JP, and it was impossible to free himself from the iron hands that were gripping him.

The guy's voice sounded familiar. Familiar and annoying. On top of his helmet he wore a bright headlight—the only source of light in the otherwise dark tunnel. The light was so blinding that Mars couldn't look directly at his kidnapper. Then when they came to an abrupt stop, Mars felt something being attached to the oxygen pack on his back.

"Hey, what are you doing?" Mars yelped in panic. There was a sweet, cold smell inside his helmet. Then everything faded to black.

Server: ad_astra
Sender: daisy_does_good_deeds
Recipients: colony_peeps
Timestamp: 2130 hours

WARNING—BREACH NEAR WEATHER TOWER. SECURE THE ENTRY!!!!!! ALL SECURITY SPECIALISTS REPORT TO CONTROL ROOM AT ONCE!!!!

Daisy Zheng

Colony Chief of Communication (CCC)

14
THE SURPRISE

Julia revved up her rover and rushed to the security wing as soon as she saw the message. When Daisy unlocked the control room door, the place was in disarray. The monitors were blinking, there were security specialists running past the desks frantically, and several kids were on their phones desperate to get information.

"There was a breach?" Julia asked.

"Worse," Daisy said. On a monitor, she showed Julia the footage of the abduction.

"You're kidding!" Julia exclaimed. She watched agog as she saw Mars being seized through a door near the weather tower entrance. "*That's* where the Martians have been getting in? We should have known!"

Julia made Daisy play the footage again, her mind racing. Of course Mars would go rushing off to find the

Martians after what she'd told him during their chess game! She should have known that, too. He'd been worrying over Aurora's disappearance for months, then he got here to the Colony, and the girl was nowhere to be found. Julia had tried her best to piece together what had happened. Even to her, something about the break-in at the greenhouse didn't sound right. There was no footage from *that*, and no evidence of a fight.

"Play that video one more time," Julia said.

"You've seen it twice."

"Third time's a charm," Julia said. She and Daisy watched again as a guy in a metallic space suit pulled Mars through the door. "Why can't we go through that door and bring Mars back?"

"We've already tried opening that door," Daisy said, "but it's no use. They've done something to it. Barricaded it on the other side."

"The Martians are stopping *us*?" Julia was incredulous. "Are you telling me they have better technology than we do?"

Daisy shrugged. "I think they just piled up a bunch of rocks."

Julia frowned. "We need to contact them. There must be a way to convince them to return Mars to us."

Daisy hesitated as her eyes met Julia's. "What if they don't want to give him up?"

🎧

Mars felt groggy as he opened his eyes. "Where am I?" he asked, sitting up.

"Welcome to the Martian Camp," said the guy in the gray metallic suit. He was seated on a stool in front of Mars, helmet off. "You sure slept like a baby. Don't get up too fast. The chloroform knocked you out last night."

"Last night?" Mars yelped. "What time is it?"

What if Daisy and Julia were looking for him?

"Relax, it's early morning. Your friends probably haven't even noticed you're gone yet," he added as if he guessed what Mars was thinking.

"Where's my helmet?" Mars started to panic, but then he calmed down. He wasn't wearing his helmet, but he seemed to be inside some kind of oxygenated space—in fact, as he looked around, it looked like they were inside an enormous bubble. "Why did you knock me out?"

The guy gave a short laugh. His hair was bleached blond with dark roots, and he wore studs in his ears. He reminded Mars of the high school Goths he saw when he went downtown, who looked all tough but then hung out at Starbucks. Only this guy didn't look like he drank lattes. Instead he looked lean and hungry, like he ate out of garbage cans.

"Easier that way," he said. "FYI, your helmet's over there." He said it without warmth, and Mars still felt like he had heard the voice before.

Mars sat up for real now even though it hurt his head.

He looked around in the dim light of the bubble. He now remembered Daisy telling him about oxy bubbles, which were portable tents that could be filled up with oxygenated air and used by up to four people overnight. "Kind of like camping," Daisy said airily. "Except if you step outside, you die!"

So they were in an oxy bubble. But where was the oxy bubble? "This is a lava tube, isn't it?" Mars guessed. "Did you carry me here?"

"Of course not. You think I can lift you, pumpkin? I brought you in a space buggy. It's parked outside the oxy bubble."

The mention of the space buggy finally reminded Mars where he had heard this voice before. "Wait a sec, you're the guy who tried to reroute our Oliver Shuttle when we first got here!"

"I didn't know I was so famous," he said, sneering. "I ought to tell Fang."

"If you know Fang, then where is Aurora?" Mars demanded. "I know you took her. You better not have hurt her. I came all the way from Earth, and I'm not leaving without her."

There was a suction sound as a flap opened and closed in the oxy bubble. The guy looked at a person standing behind Mars. "Did you hear that, Fang? He said he's not leaving."

Mars whirled around.

"Of course he isn't. He's Mars Patel." Fang's voice was distorted under an enormous battered helmet. Mars had never seen such a helmet before in the Colony. It was etched with drawings of skulls and bones and teeth, with pieces of metal encircling the top like a grim crown. Fang's ragged space suit had the same etchings, giving the sense of someone who had long been ready for battle.

Mars trembled. Would he have to fight the legendary Fang? No one even knew Mars was here. What would Daisy and Julia do if they didn't hear from him . . . like ever again?

"What did you do to her?" he said accusingly, trying to keep the fear out of his voice. He had to be brave, or how would he find Aurora?

Slowly, Fang reached up, and Mars braced himself, expecting to be struck down.

Instead, Fang pulled off the enormous helmet.

Mars almost fell down in astonishment.

"I—I don't understand . . ." he stammered.

"Surprise," Aurora said calmly. "If you don't know, now you know. I'm Fang."

FROM THE PODCAST

What happens when good guys become the bad guys?
When the people we look up to have let us down?
History is strewn with the corpses of gangsters,
phonies, and warmongers.
We live in dangerous times, my friends.
You better decide now who you're going to trust.

Mars learned the hard way when he discovered
just who Aurora REALLY is!

To the stars!

998 Comments ⊗

andromeda   25 min ago
What's going on? is OP talking war??

neptunebaby   23 min ago
It's colonists versus martians

staryoda   20 min ago
The landslides have washed away southern cal will
nobody do nothing??

allie_j 20 min ago
I'm scared #stoptherain

sandiegobeachgurl   19 min ago
Our house is gone #stoptherain

staryoda   17 min ago
full on panic #stoptherain

daisy_does_good_deeds   12 min ago
Don't worry the colonists will save ur planet and
#stoptherain

daisy_does_good_deeds   2 min ago
waitttt

15
WATCH YOUR STEP

The same day the man in the glasses came to the store, Saira Patel got in her car, filled her tank with gas, and headed inland, toward the north. It was raining there but not as much, and it was up higher than the coastline. Contrary to what the guy had said, he could *not* track her. She had installed an antiroaming device on her car so that it deflected all spyware, even by satellite. The only thing that would give her away was the IP phone Oliver had given her—but that was only if she made a call, and she never had. Not using it had kept her and Mars under an umbrella of protection. Nevertheless, she kept the phone with her always—just in case. It was traveling with her now in her glove compartment.

Even though the guy could not track her, she still traveled for days, through Northern California, and then across the Oregon border as she shifted from one motel to another. She didn't know where she was going, except that she had to keep moving. As she drove, she listened to music on the radio—to Beyoncé, Green Day, the B-52s, Taylor Swift, the Fugees, Billie Eilish, even a little Coltrane. Whatever she could find. When the radio stopped working, she stuck in her own CD of Ravi Shankar and Philip Glass. That was a good one. The music helped her think. She still wasn't sure what to do. She had been in touch with her colleagues in Mumbai only once since the rains started, and they'd decided it was too dangerous to talk—what if their call was intercepted?

One day she ended up in Bend, Oregon. She had a friend there, Meg, who was a massage therapist at one of the local resorts. They were friends from the old days, and Meg knew not to ask questions. She just let Saira crash, play with her dogs, and enjoy a free massage.

"Why don't you stay?" Meg asked. "Bend is the perfect place for no one to find you."

It was tempting. Saira stayed for several weeks, checking the data on her computer for errors, walking with Meg and the dogs along mountainous trails behind her home.

Finally, the day came. "It's been great," she told Meg. "But if I stay any longer, I'm endangering you. Also, the rains. They will come here next. You better get flood insurance."

Then Saira got in her car. This time, Seattle was on her mind, and that was the direction she headed.

As she drove, Saira thought more about the man who'd come to the store in Long Beach a few weeks before. How had he managed to find her? It had unnerved her. That was the chief reason she'd gotten in her car and fled. Also, why on earth did he look so familiar? Not only that, something about his face evoked a sense of sheepishness in her, a memory of someone, her or Mars getting in trouble and . . .

A few seconds later she almost slammed her brakes. That was it! That man was the detention teacher in Mars's school. She couldn't remember his name. Schwartz? Quartz? What was *he* doing chasing after the data? Was he working for Oliver? Or against him?

Saira was an hour outside Seattle at a gas station when she heard the glass-shattering sound from her phone. A new podcast! She finished filling the tank and pulled the car off to the side of the parking lot.

There he was, Oliver being his usual annoying self. Blah, blah. And then he said something that made her gasp: *Mars learned the hard way when he discovered just who Aurora really is!*

Could Mars have reached the Colony? With Aurora? A vision of that girl with the purple-tipped hair and spiky wristbands came to her mind—the one Mars hung around with all the time, the one who'd turned his head and changed everything for him. But it wasn't just Aurora that filled her mind. Everything else was starting to make sense. Mars gone. Aurora gone. The other missing kids at home. Gone.

Saira leaned back in her seat. *"Main kya karoon?"* she said unhappily. What should she do?

Those parents' faces haunted her. They had all banded together. They had posted flyers, combed the Internet for clues, begged the Port Elizabeth police to do something—*anything*. Then finally they had come as a group to her door. One of them looked Saira in the eye and started to cry. "Even if you can't save yours, please save mine," she begged. "He's my only child."

Saira almost cried with the woman. "Mars is my only child, too," she said as gently as she could. "But I cannot help you. I don't know where your son is."

That was half a year ago. Why hadn't she realized it before—that Oliver Pruitt was the reason all along? As one parent to another, she felt a duty to find out. All it would take was a single phone call.

She reached into the glove compartment. For a long moment she looked at the oblong silver case in her lap. She had been dying to use the IP phone. In just a few seconds, she might be able to speak to Mars. To find out how he was, where he was, and when—if—he was coming back. Every time the temptation had driven her nearly mad, she'd put the phone away.

Well, she was done with running away.

Saira looked out the window to where the dark sky obscured the sun. What she would give for a warm, sunny day from her childhood in Mumbai. Running on the sand at Chowpatty Beach, stopping to buy an ear of roasted corn sprinkled with chaat masala, smelling the pungent salt-sea air, like no other place in the world. Then she took a deep breath and dialed the number to the Colony.

It took forever to hear the voice on the other side. It was the voice of young person, a girl.

Saira had to be quick. She might only have a few minutes to spare.

"Hello, this Saira Patel," she said. "I need to talk to my son, Mars."

And just like that, came the rat-tat-tat sound of a chopper approaching in the distance.

16
LIVE TO SPY

You're Fang? *You're* Fang?" Mars couldn't stop repeating himself. "But . . . all this time, I thought you were in trouble!"

"I *was* in trouble, Mars," Aurora said. "Oliver Pruitt lied to me, to all of us." Her hand swept behind her where the rest of the Martians were in the lava tube, watching them sullenly from outside the oxy bubble. With a shock, Mars realized they had surrounded the bubble in the last few minutes after Aurora had entered. "We're starving, we're tired, and we want to go back home to Earth."

"Yeah!" Mars could hear voices outside, muttering angrily in agreement.

"But why didn't you stay at the Colony?" Mars asked. "There's food there. And the other kids. Everything seems to be going good there. They're building new stuff, and—"

"*And?* Pruitt controls everything. We're living underground like rats next to a volcano, eating frozen food and meet burgers. No sunlight, no fresh air, trapped like sardines. This isn't the solution to our problems on Earth. This is just a new nightmare we're living. Am I right, Axel?"

The guy in the metallic suit nodded. "The place sucks. We gotta bring it down. *That's* the solution."

Mars looked uncertainly from Aurora to this guy, Axel, to the kids surrounding them outside the bubble. They all *did* look miserable. No one looked washed or fed. And if a savvy person like Aurora couldn't figure out how to live in the Colony, then where did that leave Mars?

"Aurora, I hear what you're saying . . ." he said slowly. "And I agree that the Colony wasn't exactly what I thought it would be."

"Look at you, Mars," Aurora said suddenly. "Did you leave your mom and your friends to be cleaning up tardigrade poop? Great job that is!"

Mars flushed. How did Aurora know about that? He remembered the camera in the tunnel. "Aurora, does Oliver Pruitt . . . spy on us?"

She started laughing. "Oh, Mars! You're a scream. Do you know that every tunnel in the Colony has lines of tiny cameras installed at the top? The cameras are shatterproof, smudgeproof, and wireless. They work by satellite, even underground. And they're coated with a zinc sulfide dye. You can't touch them or you'll start to glow."

"But . . ." Mars said in disbelief. "Why?"

"Because Pruitt lives to spy. Because he's super paranoid about everything."

"First thing we do when we get to the Colony is destroy all the cameras," Axel said.

Aurora shook her head. "First, we get off this planet. We don't have time for anything else."

"You're serious, aren't you?" Mars said slowly. He watched Aurora toss her hair back. It was no longer purple on the ends—instead, she had dyed the tips black—but that gesture was the same. He knew it from the first day of sixth grade. The memories had come flooding back. This was Aurora for real. And yet . . .

"I don't know, Aurora. All of this is going so fast. I mean . . ." he faltered. "Did you even get all my texts? Did you know what was going on when you were missing on Earth?"

"Of course I did." Aurora watched him for a moment and her face softened. "Axel, can you give us a moment? In private?"

Axel made a face and sauntered off to stand near the flap, staring malevolently at the kids outside. He certainly seemed angry.

Aurora drew Mars over to a side. "I got all of your texts, Mars. And . . ." She stopped. She suddenly leaned over and wrapped her arms around him. "Ouch. Kinda hard to hug a space suit. But you know I really missed you, right?"

Mars flushed. "Yeah," he whispered. He'd missed her, too. No one else had ever made him feel the way she did. Like the two of them could rule the school. All those pranks, all those hours in detention. There was a power in that, in knowing they didn't need the approval of Clyde Boofsky, or any of the awful kids in their grade. But now sixth grade seemed so long ago. Would he ever feel that way again?

"Like, I can't believe you came all this way just to find me, Mars," she said. "It means a lot. More than you know."

"I promised I'd be here for you, Aurora," he said.

She nodded. "I know, Mars."

That last time he'd seen her in the school parking lot, she was crying, her mascara running under her eyes. Now she wasn't wearing makeup. Her face had grown hard and lean, and for a moment, Mars worried that Aurora had been marked forever by this ordeal. Was she still the same person? She took off her glove to grasp his sleeve. He did the same, and their hands touched. It seemed like she was the same Aurora. She had to be.

"So, like, um, the gang—they're OK? And your mom?" she asked.

"I don't really know," he said. "I haven't heard anything since I left."

"See? Isn't that a reason to get back? For them?"

"I guess," Mars said uncertainly.

Of course he wanted to go back home, but something in Aurora's tone made him uncomfortable. It was like in Port Elizabeth when she would tell her mom on the phone that she was at Mars's place, and they were actually downtown having milkshakes. It wasn't the lying that bothered Mars, but how she would go on and on about how much studying she was getting done. There was lying and there was faking.

Above them the lights flickered off, and the sound of the generator shut off. Around them was a collective groan.

"What happened?" Mars asked nervously.

"There goes the generator again," Aurora said stonily.

"You have a generator?"

"Sure. How else do you think we keep this place lit and heated?" She turned on a flashlight and reached for something that looked like toolbox. "I'll go, Axel. You man the bubble. Come on, Mars. Walk with me. But put on your helmet and gloves first." She slipped on her gloves and pulled on her own helmet, and they walked out of the flap using a flashlight. "This way," she said as they walked past Martian kids huddling outside the oxy bubble. "No going in the bubble or you'll have to answer to Axel."

Mars followed Aurora, watching in surprise as the kids murmured to one another but stayed where they were. "Why can't they go in?" he asked as they kept walking.

"Are you kidding me? You know how hard it was to steal that oxy bubble? It's like our mission control. That's where we keep all our equipment, tools, stuff. Also if someone gets sick, we bring them there to recover. Otherwise it's the lava tube for everyone. Even me."

"Oh," Mars said.

A few minutes later, Aurora and he reached a small generator resting on a slab of stone. Aurora put down her tool kit. "Hold the flashlight, will you?" she asked, then rummaged through the kit while he shone the light.

"You know what to do?" he asked, taken aback. "Aren't generators kinda dangerous?"

"Nah, this one's small, and it's probably a spark plug that needs to be replaced. I have a bunch of them I stole along with this generator from the supply room. Just shine the light over here." She used a wrench as she continued. "You'd be surprised, Mars, all the stuff I've learned."

"Not really," Mars said. "I always knew you were smart."

"I *am* smart," Aurora said. She gave a final turn of the wrench. "That ought to do it. Stand back." She pressed a button, and the generator came to life as lights turned on down the lava tube.

"Awesome, Aurora," Mars said. He marveled at how she'd just fixed a piece of equipment that the Martians were literally depending on to survive.

"Try telling that to Pruitt." She grabbed the toolbox and

started walking back as Mars scrambled to follow her. "You see, I thought he brought me here to be somebody, to *do* things," she said. "But I wasn't special. I was just a lure to get you. You must be pretty special if Pruitt wants you here so bad."

"But Aurora . . ." Mars said. "You're also—"

"Don't you see, Mars? I have no purpose here. It's kind of like it was back in Port Elizabeth. Every day, same thing. Go to school, come home. My mom MIA most of the time, doing that crappy waitress job at the Buckets Diner. Like, who would even eat at a place called Buckets? And then even though I got As on all my tests, the teachers had it in for me. Because of some stupid attendance problem. Why should I come to class if I get As without being there?"

"I know, right?" Mars said. "It only got worse after you left."

"Yeah, well that was Port Elizabeth. It was supposed to be better here. But it's not! The Colony operates the same way, except it isn't school; it's worse. You're expected to work all the time, you don't get paid, and you don't get a say in how anything is done unless you're one of the kiss-up Colonists like Daisy or Orion. So being here, my life is ruined. And if I try to leave, I can either get radiation sickness and die an awful death, or run out of air and ditto. Or I could get stomped by a tardigrade. All these fun ways to die!"

"Wow," Mars said slowly. "I guess you're right." Aurora

had this way of making everything sound completely different from what he'd thought. Was the Colony really *that* awful? After all, Daisy, Julia, and Orion were doing a pretty good job. Of course, that didn't change the fact that Oliver Pruitt had tricked everyone one way or another.

"That's why you have to help me get home to Earth, Mars," Aurora said suddenly. "I have to get my life back. I'm counting on you."

Mars stared at her, surprised. "How am I going to do that? I haven't even seen Oliver Pruitt for real yet. And I don't know how to fly."

"But you could help us get on a shuttle back to the space station. That's what we were trying to do that day when we rerouted your flight. We wanted the shuttle. Axel figured he could program the autopilot to go in reverse. But then you crashed."

"And survived!" Mars looked at her carefully. Had she forgotten that part where he and Julia almost died?

"Of course," Aurora said automatically. She paused for a millisecond, then went plowing ahead. "But now we *need* to get on that last shuttle at the Colony."

"You mean the Lifeboat?" Mars asked doubtfully. "That only fits four people. And you have to fly it manually. Nobody knows how to do that except Orion, and Julia, who he just trained. But Orion has gone back to the space station, and there's NO way Julia will fly you."

"I wouldn't be so sure," Aurora said. "She will if she wants something we have."

By now they had reached the oxy bubble. Axel, who was still standing guard, saw them and leered. "So is the golden boy on board?" he asked.

"Golden boy?" Mars repeated. Why did everyone have a nickname for him?

"Your plan better work, Fang," Axel said, ignoring Mars.

"Oh, our plan will work," Aurora said calmly. "This is Mars Patel, and he would do anything for me. Right, Mars?"

"Sure," Mars said uncomfortably. There was that tone in Aurora's voice again. "Wait a sec, what plan?"

Just then, one of the Martian kids came running to them holding up an IP phone.

"Fang," he cried. "They've found us!"

17
A GOOD REASON

Julia, wait!" Daisy said, standing in front of the monitors in the control room. She and Julia had taken turns staying up that night, watching for any sign of the door opening on the surveillance video. It was now early morning and the gold ribbons Daisy had woven in her hair had come undone, making her look like she was coming undone, too.

"Not now, Daisy." Julia's face was suspended over a microphone set up at one of the desks. "I've found the Martians' signal. I'm in!"

"But Julia . . ." Daisy said more insistently, waving a phone in her hand.

"Quiet, Daisy. Hello, hello? This is Colony Control. Do you read me? Is this Fang? And the Martians? Over."

There was an audible click. "Yeah, this is Fang. We hear you. What do you want? Over." There was another click. "No, wait. We have someone here. I bet you want to know. Over."

Julia rolled her eyes. "Of course we already know, Fang. We know all your pathetic tricks. Now listen, we want Mars back. Put him on the phone. We haven't heard from him since last night. We need to know he's fine. Over."

There was laughter on the other side. "You think you call the shots, Julia, but you don't. I'll put Mars on the line so he can tell you what *we* want. Over."

"Julia, this can't wait anymore!" Daisy cried out right as Mars got on the phone. "I have Mars's mother on the other line! She wants to talk to him NOW."

"My mom?" Mars's voice pitched high. "Julia, what's going on? My mom's on the phone? I need to talk to her."

Julia pursed her lips. Things were getting crazier. "OK, patch her through, Daisy."

Daisy went to the switchboard, and suddenly a voice burst through the speakers.

"Mars? Mars?" Saira Patel sounded urgent. "Is that you?"

"Ma! Oh my god. It's really you!"

"I waited so long, beta."

"I'm so sorry, Mamaji."

For several seconds, there was incoherent blabbering on both ends.

"Mars, Mars, you need to listen to me," Saira Patel cut in. "I can't talk for long. I have important information for you. Your friends Caddie, JP, and Toothpick are gone."

"Gone?" Mars repeated. "Where did they go?"

"Missing!" Her voice was getting clipped. "They never came back after you left. Their parents are desperate. I need to know. If Aurora made it to Mars, did your friends? Did they—"

Suddenly, her voice was cut off.

"Ma!" Mars yelled. "Ma!" His voice turned frantic. "Why isn't she talking? What's going on?"

"Daisy, hurry—flip to another channel," Julia instructed.

Daisy kept tapping the switchboard. "It's no use, we've lost audio."

Mars was still yelling on his end. "Where are my friends? What's going on? Oh my god, Oliver Pruitt said they would be safe. And now they're missing, too!"

There was a heated conversation on Mars's side. Then the phone was wrested from him.

"I'm back!" It was Fang. "You can see for yourself. Mars is here, alive and well. But now we need something from the Colony. We need for you, Julia, to take me, Axel, and Mars back to the space station. Immediately!"

"Why in the universe would I do something like that?" Julia demanded.

"Reason one: you're the only one who can fly the Lifeboat. Orion isn't around, and Daisy can't fly manual. Reason two: you're going to do it if you want to see Mars again."

Julia's voice hardened. "Let's get one thing straight, Fang Face. I don't negotiate with terrorists. That's what you are. You're going to bring Mars over, or you and your Martian friends can go starve yourselves. You're nothing without our supplies. Well, try stealing them now! We know where you're getting in. We're guarding it twenty-four/seven. And Daisy has ordered a special airlock to be constructed for that entry that only opens on one side. On *our* side."

Daisy gave her a surprised look, but Julia held a finger to her lips.

"I think that's where you're seriously wrong, Julia," Fang said. "Mars has about thirty minutes of oxygen left in his suit. If we don't come to an agreement, I think Mars can say goodbye to oxygenated air."

There was a loud note of dissent on the other side. Then Mars came back on the line. "Julia, I'm sorry. I don't like the way this is being handled. But everything has changed. You heard my mom. You have to take us to the space station."

"Mars, are you hurt? Do you need medical help?" Julia asked anxiously.

"It's not me. It's my friends. They're missing, and I need to find Oliver Pruitt. We have to make him answer to us."

"But Mars . . ."

"I know you don't talk to terrorists. But Fang isn't a terrorist. Trust me. You need to do this for me. What's the point of kids running a colony if we don't do it right?"

Daisy looked stricken. "Julia, this is ransom!" She was quivering from head to toe in her neon blue bodysuit. "You can't say yes. IT GOES AGAINST THE RULES!"

Julia debated. Daisy was right. The Colony depended on rules. It was rules that had built the domes, pressurized the tunnels, designed the weather surveillance system, and ensured that the produce was safe to harvest and eat. The rules had kept them alive on a planet that would otherwise kill them. But it was Butterfly, and he had not abandoned her when the Oliver Shuttle crashed and the Martians were coming for them. He was in their clutches now, yet he was still putting his friends first. "I'm sorry, Daisy," Julia said. "But sometimes we have to break the rules."

18
LIFEBOAT

The Lifeboat shuttle was docked at the flight platform, ever ready for action. In addition to launching all the Oliver Shuttles, it was one of Daisy's many jobs to see that the Lifeboat was always primed to go. But Daisy had never launched the Lifeboat, because the Lifeboat had never been used. It was designed for an emergency, which so far had never happened. Until now.

Nervously, Daisy helped everyone get suited up for the flight: Mars, Axel, Julia, and Fang—or Aurora, as everyone discovered when the motley crew reached the South Dome and took off their helmets.

"*You're* Fang?" Daisy uttered in disbelief. "But you were doing so well in the greenhouse."

"Why am I not surprised?" Julia said coolly, staring hard at Aurora.

Aurora glared back. "Really, Daisy, do you think I came here to grow lettuce?"

"But . . . but," Daisy said helplessly. She couldn't understand why anyone would trade the experience of living in the Colony for . . . she looked more closely at Aurora's scruffy space suit. Was that a skull-and-bones symbol carved into the helmet? Next to Aurora, Axel was already defacing the side of the dome wall with a marker.

"Let's go, everyone," Mars said, walking ahead of them. "If we're doing this, let's do it."

By now, everyone was pretty much glaring at everyone else. Julia was pissed off, Axel was up to no good, Aurora was sneering, and Mars was unhappy at being "the ransom guy."

But clearly *she* was the unhappiest, Daisy decided, as she led them to the suit room. That's because she was prepared for everything . . . except a real disaster. And Aurora and Axel on the Lifeboat without authorization was the gravest disaster of all. Because Daisy knew the true cost of getting it wrong on Mars—mayhem and destruction! What if Aurora's brash decision destroyed them all?

Getting everyone into their flight suits and helmets took nearly an hour. There was so much equipment, and it had to be worn correctly to ensure a proper seal. Plus, Axel fidgeted, and Aurora refused to change out of the suit she was wearing. "This is premium Martian gear," she said, smirking, even when Mars pleaded with her to change into a new space suit that would offer better protection. Eventually he gave up, and Aurora continued to look like death in her skull-and-bones decor.

Finally, when everyone was ready, Daisy reluctantly led them through the airlock and onto the shuttle platform. By now, Daisy's hair was way beyond limp, the gold ribbons had fallen away, and there was glitter smeared across her face. She was a sad mess.

"Daisy, close the hatch, will ya?" Aurora said leaning back in her seat. "Oooh, I'm gonna like this ride!"

"Strap in," Axel said. "We are going to PAR-TAY."

"Yeehaw," crowed Aurora.

Daisy reached for the hatch. "To the stars," she said, faltering. Disappointment welled through her. How would she look Mr. Pruitt in the eye? Aurora and Axel—they were the worst kind of Colonist, not thinking of anyone but themselves. Now Daisy was left behind to clean up the mess, only how would she ever do it? So many of the Colonists depended on her. The Renewable Oxygen Group, the Composting Club, the Young Innovators Society, the lunch crew, the list went on. And now she was getting an alert from the weather tower on her IP phone.

"Daisy, there's something odd," said Mica, one of the weather technicians. "I think—"

"Not now, Mica," Daisy said, distracted. "I'll call you back. Over and out." She tugged at the hatch.

"Chin up, Daisy," Julia said, as she and Mars slid past and entered the spacecraft.

Daisy nodded mutely and closed the hatch behind them.

🎧

Inside the shuttle, Julia followed behind Mars and went straight to the control panel.

"Julia, you're amazing, flying the Lifeboat," Mars told her. "I don't know how you do it."

"I don't know *why* I do it," she muttered as she entered coordinates into the flight console.

While Julia prepared for takeoff, Mars looked at Axel and Aurora. Axel was already asleep, his head tipped back, snoring softly.

Aurora's eyes met Mars's. "He's tired. Nobody really gets much sleep in the lava tubes. We don't, like, have real beds. This chair is probably the most comfy thing Axel's been in for a while."

"What about you? Why aren't you conking out?"

Aurora pinched her lips. "So I can keep an eye on the two of you. How do I know you and Julia aren't going to secretly conspire against me?"

"Geez, Aurora, way to be paranoid," Mars said, feeling hurt. "Especially when we're doing everything you wanted."

"We're doing what *you* wanted, Mars." Aurora's voice held its same bitterness. "You don't get it. I have to fight for everything. People don't hand things to me on a platter."

"People don't hand things to me either," Mars said. "And JP, Toothpick, and Caddie are your friends, too. Don't you want to know what happened to them?"

"Of course I do," Aurora said. "I told you already. Oliver Pruitt is an evil liar. You can't trust him. Maybe they're prisoners back at Pruitt Prep. And that dork Mr. Q is watching them in some Pruitt detention class." She snickered. She seemed more relaxed now that they were no longer in the lava tubes.

"I'm serious, Aurora," Mars said. "I'm worried about my mom, too. I didn't even get to speak to her much. Did something happen? Why did she get cut off like that?"

Aurora softened. "Yeah. Look, maybe it was just a bad connection. She sounded more worried about you. She's a great mom. I know just from the way you talk about her. She must really love you. I wish that . . ." She stopped, her voice trailing off. "I bet my mom isn't even looking for me."

"That's not true."

Aurora shrugged it off. "I still want to go home. Even if I don't need her or my dad."

Mars wanted to say something, but he didn't know what. Aurora had always had a weird relationship with her parents.

"OK, ready for takeoff," Julia announced.

"Next stop, Pruitt's face," Aurora said.

With a roar, the Lifeboat slid out of the docking station.

Server: ad_astra
Sender: daisy_does_good_deeds
Recipients: colony_peeps
Timestamp: 0600 hours

Hi Colony Peeps,

This message is to inform you that the Lifeboat has been dispatched on a top-secret perilous mission. Meanwhile, we need all hands on deck to maintain discipline and order, and to secure any nonauthorized entries into the Colony. That means weird-looking doors without a door handle!! The Colony is depending on you. Also reminder: please refrain from throwing out old game boards into the food scraps bin. The kitchen staff found chess pieces along with the potato skins. Seriously, folks!

Finally, if you could, please wish Godspeed to the Lifeboat's aforementioned top-secret mission. I hate not being able to to talk to them!

To the stars!
Daisy Zheng
Colony Chief of Communication (CCC)

∩

It came as no surprise that Julia was an expert flying the shuttle, even her first time. And because they weren't imminently crashing, Mars had a chance to look out the observation window. Which was good because it helped him not think about the things that Aurora had been saying and doing. Had she always been so . . . difficult?

From the window he saw the Colony below, a lone hub in the middle of an endless stretch of reddish, desolate land. It swiftly receded, and then all he saw was the red land itself, a series of sandy dunes, layered rock, and cracked lines cutting into the surface, suggesting a time when water flowed on the surface of the planet. There was Mount Olympus, the volcano that made him think of home, and next to it Monument Crater, immense and shadowy, the site of Julia and Mars's crash landing. Then the volcano, the crater, and all traces of the planet faded away as the Lifeboat broke through the atmosphere.

Next to him, Aurora had also fallen silent, looking at the same view. He wondered if she was thinking the same thing, too, how unreal and incredible it was seeing the Red Planet from up here. Except she was planning to leave it behind forever. Would Oliver Pruitt finally hear her out? Would he allow Aurora and Axel to go home? And where were Caddie, JP, and Toothpick? There were so many unknowns, and they were all making him anxious.

Soon the Lifeboat was pulling into the space station. Mars thought back to when he first arrived with Julia and Orion, how he was so sure the Martians were waiting to ambush him. Now he was coming back with two of them on board. "You never know," he said out loud, echoing what Daisy liked to say.

"Huh?" Aurora asked. She crossed and uncrossed her arms, restless in her space suit.

When the Lifeboat was fully docked, Julia instructed everyone to put on their helmets just in case there was some issue with pressurization as they exited the spacecraft. Aurora poked Axel awake, and then the four disembarked, with Mars taking up the rear. On their way out, he helped Julia stow her rover.

"Goodbye for now, dear rover," she said as Mars closed the hatch. "How I will miss you."

"It's not like a person," Axel said snidely, hearing her.

Julia wrinkled her nose. "If only people were *half* as reliable as a rover," she retorted.

∩

Outside the shuttle, now that they were no longer strapped down, everyone felt the familiar buoy of weightlessness pull them up. Julia floated ahead as Aurora giggled for the first time that day and Axel pinwheeled in the air, grinning.

"Hey, not bad," Aurora called out to Julia. "You didn't kill us."

"Don't give me ideas," Julia returned, glowering.

"Come on guys, hurry," Mars said to them. He was starting to get uneasy again as he thought over what his mom had told him over the phone back at the Colony. What did she mean when she said his friends were missing? Why did she think he would know where they were?

"Hey, it's that robot," Axel noticed. "Look."

"You mean HELGA," Mars said.

"Welcome to Pruitt Space Station," said HELGA, who was waiting on the platform. "I am HELGA, your transit assistant. You have made an unauthorized arrival. Your identity will need to be verified before you can access the main cabin."

"Yo, HELGA, it's us," Mars said. "Remember, you saw us, like, a month ago?"

"I'm sorry, I do not know how to yo-yo. But you can upgrade my system to upload a module on games and magic tricks."

"No, HELGA," Mars said impatiently. "I'm saying hi because we've met you before."

"I will scan previous passenger lists," HELGA said. "One moment please. Yes. Confirmation completed for Mars Patel, Julia Morrell-Cole, Aurora Gershowitz, and Axel Thunderbolt."

"That's not your real name, is it?" Mars asked, surprised

"Ha, ha. You'll never know," Axel said. "Why is the

garbage can following us? Hey, we can take it from here, Spy Can."

"I am not spyware or a receptacle for trash," HELGA said pleasantly. "I am your transit assistant. You have made an unauthorized arrival to Pruitt Space Station. Please state your purpose."

"We're here to see Oliver Pruitt," Mars said. "So where is he?"

"Mr. Pruitt is unavailable to take your visit," HELGA told them.

Aurora stopped. "Why is that? He's too good for us?"

HELGA's mouth went in that strange upward U that was supposed to be a smile but looked more like a malfunction. "That is known as a false equivalency. His goodness is independent of your goodness. You cannot see him because he is not here."

Aurora looked like she was ready to explode. "What? Where is he?"

"Mr. Pruitt has departed on that shuttle." HELGA's steel arm pointed toward one of the windows, where they could see the flames of a departing shuttle becoming smaller and smaller.

"No way!" Mars was stunned.

"That's going in the direction of Mars," Julia observed.

"I thought there were only two shuttles left," Axel said. "Is that a lie?"

"There are two shuttles left for Colony use," HELGA said. "This excludes Mr. Pruitt's personal shuttle."

"I don't believe it," Aurora thundered. "He must have known we were coming."

"Also," HELGA continued, "Mr. Pruitt has set the space station to self-destruct in ten minutes."

"I beg your pardon!" Julia said, aghast. "You're telling us this space station is going to explode while we're on it?"

"I don't want to die!" Axel screeched.

"That settles it," Julia said. "We're leaving."

"But we still don't know where Caddie, JP, and Toothpick are," Mars said. "I came here to find out."

"It's too late," Julia said. "We need to get back on the Lifeboat. There's just enough fuel to get us back to the Colony."

"Wait a minute. I am NOT going back to the Colony," Aurora fumed. "I want to go back to Earth."

"Be reasonable," Julia said. "We have exactly ten minutes before this station implodes and we're zapped into fine particulate matter. I'm getting back on the Lifeboat."

"I'm with Julia," Axel said immediately.

Meanwhile, Mars was still mulling over his mom's phone call. She'd seemed to think that if Aurora was with him, then the rest of his friends were, too. But how was that possible? Unless . . .

"The cargo hold," Mars said suddenly. He was surprised

he had never thought of it before. "That's where they are."

"Who?" Julia asked. "Wait, your friends?"

"Why else would Oliver Pruitt be so secretive and not let me in there?" Mars said. "HELGA, where did the cargo delivery go?"

"It was transferred to this room here," HELGA said, pointing to a set of double doors opening right to the platform.

"Open it for us," Mars said urgently.

"You do not have the authorization," HELGA said sweetly.

Mars groaned. "C'mon, HELGA, we need you to open it. The space station is about to explode."

"Mars, they can't still be in there," Julia said. "It was three weeks ago."

"I need to check," Mars insisted.

"I think we need to get on the Lifeboat," Axel interrupted.

"Oh my god," Aurora said. "This is, like, so unfair."

"Do something, somebody," Mars said helplessly.

Julia leaned over to HELGA. "There must be an emergency provision on this robot. Look, here it is." She pressed a yellow button at the base of HELGA's neck.

"You have activated my emergency adaptive circuit," HELGA informed them.

"I command you to open the cargo room," Julia said. "Before the station explodes."

HELGA obliged by inputting some numbers into a keypad on the wall.

Silently the double doors slid open to reveal a dimly lit room.

"It worked!" Mars rushed in.

The small room was cramped and filled wall-to-wall with computerized equipment: LCD screens, cables, several CPUs stacked on top of one another, and at the center, three very large pods, hooked up with wiring to the CPUs. There were fans blowing in the room, and the sound of beeping. Mars looked more closely and saw that the beeping came from monitors, which were measuring the amount of oxygen being supplied to each pod. Oxygen?

"Oh my god," Mars said. "Guys, help me pry these pods open before it's too late!"

Julia paled. "Come on, all hands on deck. We've got approximately five minutes."

"No, four," HELGA corrected.

By now, Mars had undone the lid to the first pod, his fingers fumbling with the latches. He was scared he would run out of time. But when he flipped back the lid, he drew in his breath, because inside the pod, time had stopped. Well, almost.

Her hair was still chestnut brown, though it was longer, and the ends had curled. Her glasses were the ones she had worn at the dance, the ones with the glittery flames, and they were perched on her nose. The flannel coat she wore still smelled of pine and fabric softener. She was the same. She was incredibly the same. Her eyes fluttered open and she was . . . Caddie.

19
THE GETAWAY THAT GOT AWAY

When Caddie Patchett opened her eyes after seven long months of induced hibernation, the last thing she expected to hear was that she was on a space station that was about to explode.

"What?" she murmured groggily. "I need a minute."

"You have three," said Mars. "I mean, it's GREAT to see you, Cads! But we have to get out of here NOW."

Overhead an alarm notification sounded.

"WARNING: THIS SPACE STATION IS SCHEDULED FOR SELF-DETONATION IN THREE MINUTES. PREPARE TO EVACUATE."

Caddie felt the twin sensations of fear and sluggishness assail her. Mars! Was that really him . . . in a space suit? Through a fog, she heard similar bursts of relief and confusion. "You have no idea." "You guys are awesome!" "What on earth are you doing here?" "Hurry!" If only Caddie could explain everything. If only she could get her arms and legs to work the way they should.

Somehow she managed to climb out of the sleep pod. Nearby, JP was stirring awake, and so was Toothpick, his pet drone, Droney, still clutched tightly in his arms. Wait—were they floating in the air? Was this the thing they had learned about in science class? Zero gravity? Being Jell-O? Caddie felt Mars grab her as another girl did the same with Toothpick, and Aurora with JP. Aurora?

"Aurora, oh my god, is that you?" JP mumbled, struggling to keep their eyes open.

"The one and only," Aurora said. "It's your lucky day."

Everyone rushed toward the Lifeboat with their still-awakening friends in tow. The alarm continued to blare, counting down the minutes.

Now only two.

On the platform, Mars pointed out a huge problem. "None of them have suits!"

Before he could say another word, HELGA sailed up to them. "Mars, please find spare space suits waiting here for your three friends. You can have them outfitted in sixty seconds."

"HELGA!" Mars exclaimed. "You rock!"

"Actually, I am a fully automated computer device," HELGA said.

"Whoa," JP murmured.

Then each person was hastily stuffed into a suit, zippered up, levels checked, helmets on, and loaded into the Lifeboat. It was remarkable, considering how long it had taken in the Colony. Fear of death seemed to make everything go faster.

Then they discovered another problem, this time with the Lifeboat.

"Hey, there's only room for four," Axel said

"We'll make it work," Julia said. "I'll fly us out of here."

"You fly?" Caddie said, dazed. But there was no time for anyone to explain anything. Things were *happening*.

"Everyone squeeze together," Mars ordered as they repositioned themselves inside the cramped capsule. There would be no strapping in, just holding on to one another and hoping for the best.

At the command module, Julia entered the coordinates for the return journey.

"Hold on for dear life," she said. "Mars, close the hatch."

As Mars went through the airlock and reached for the hatch, HELGA hovered quietly on the platform.

"To the stars," HELGA said in her same pleasant tone.

"HELGA—wait," Mars said. "We can't leave her here."

"Mars, she's a robot," Aurora said. "There's no room for her."

"Yeah, forget about her," Axel said.

By now, Caddie found her thinking was getting more clear, less groggy.

"That doesn't sound right," she said.

"She's a teachable unit," said Toothpick, who had found his voice, too, "like Droney." He looked at the electronic drone resting in his arms, still in hibernation mode.

Mars gestured to the robot. "Come on, HELGA. We'll make room."

HELGA's U smile wavered.

"I cannot jeopardize your mission," she said. "I am your transit assistant, programmed to make your stay pleasant and convenient."

"Well, our stay is about to detonate in thirty seconds," Mars said. "I command you on board!"

HELGA floated toward the open hatch. "This is unauthorized and unprecedented."

"You're in emergency mode, remember?" Julia said. "But do hurry!"

Everyone groaned, feeling their space suits press up against one another as HELGA squeezed in.

"Hatch closed," Mars yelled and sealed the airlock door behind him.

"Three, two, one!" Julia announced.

There was a blast of amazing proportions—so loud it was impossible to know which was bigger, the sound of the

Lifeboat zooming out of the station, or the station exploding to smithereens.

"Aaaaaaaah!" came the collective sound from everyone.

Then the shuttle stabilized. And the crew.

From the small window, they watched smoking debris and pieces of steel floating in the ether.

"It's so sad," Caddie said. "Why would Oliver Pruitt do it?"

"The space station took ten years to build," Toothpick said. "I watched a YouTube video on it."

"Why would someone destroy their life's work like that?" JP said. "This blows. But so does Oliver Pruitt."

"Oh my god, yes," Aurora said. "Someone finally gets it!"

"According to Mr. Pruitt, several private companies were planning to travel to the space station," HELGA said. "It was reported that this added competition would have threatened the mission."

"Are you saying he destroyed the station to keep people away?" JP asked. "That's so twisted."

"Twisted: I do not understand this expression of contortion," HELGA said. "But yes. To keep people away. This includes Mars Patel and his friends. Mr. Pruitt could not take any chances."

"Any chances with what?" Caddie asked.

"That I do not know," HELGA said. "I am only sharing overheard information." She paused to look at Mars. "Please permit me to thank you for saving my circuits."

Mars smiled. "Of course. Friends don't leave friends behind. You're our friend. I mean, you're also a CPU, but that's OK."

"Hmm . . . there's something daffy going on here," Julia said from the control panel.

"Daffy?" Aurora said. "Is that, like, some British expression?"

"No, it's not a *British* expression," Julia said crossly. "It's a *Julia* one. Something's not working here. At first I thought it's because I'm flying manual. But that's not it. When I try to accelerate, I get nothing. After the initial blast that got us out of here, it's like we're literally floating. Oh my god." Julia stopped.

"What? What?" JP asked. "Wait, hold the phone. Are you the same Julia? Like Lost in London?"

"Pleased to make your acquaintance," Julia said, "but excuse me if I tell you that we have some excrement hitting the fan right now."

"The thrust," Toothpick said. "We've lost the thrust."

"How did you know?" Julia asked. "That was my same conclusion."

"The initial blast is what gave us the momentum to jettison out," Toothpick said. "But now we have no independent energy to keep us going. Was the Lifeboat damaged? Or maybe it's a fuel issue."

"Yes," Julia said sadly. "I made a grave error. Now I see

that the fuel meter reset after I restarted the shuttle. We're on empty!"

"What does that mean?" Aurora said. "English, please."

"It means we're out of fuel, Aurora," Caddie said. "Like on the highway. What happens when you run out of gas?"

"Somebody rescues you," Axel said. "Like, me and my brother were driving on Route 50 and we ran out of gas. We had to wait for the gas station to come refuel us."

"No gas station here," JP said, "and nobody to rescue us."

There was a silence.

"Great," Axel said finally. "We're gonna die here after all."

∩

Pandemonium ensued. Mostly it was wailing from Axel, Aurora, and JP. But then slowly they started to calm down. First of all, there was barely any room inside the capsule, which meant it was better to sit still. Second, Julia and Toothpick had already put their heads together. No fuel meant no thrust. But no thrust didn't mean they were completely out of options. Yet.

Meanwhile, Aurora started listing all the reasons she hated Oliver Pruitt, the Colony, life on Mars, and people in general: sneaky, weird, bad food, bad company, nowhere to go, and nowhere to be.

"Sucks," she said. "All of it."

"That bad?" JP said, sympathizing. "But hey, I'm tripping you're here. Like, we finally rescued you!"

"Rescued? Ha, ha," Aurora said. "But thanks, JP. I'm tripping to see you, too."

Mars and Caddie were next to each other, and so far neither of them seemed to know what to say. They were both acting strangely shy.

Mars started. "I didn't think I would see you again, Caddie."

"I know," Caddie agreed. "Remember the dance? It was only seven months ago, but we were different. More innocent, maybe?"

Mars remembered sneaking into the middle school gym that night and seeing Caddie dressed up for the first time. It wasn't just that she looked so pretty, but she looked like she was in charge.

"We *were* different," he said. "I think it's because now we know more. Though there's one thing I wish I'd known sooner—that you were with us on the spaceship."

"We didn't even know until it happened," Caddie said. "When Mr. Q offered to let us come, too, he said we needed to be asleep. To save on resources. But it was an easy decision. We all really wanted to go."

"So why didn't anyone tell me?" Mars asked. "Why did Oliver keep it a secret?"

Caddie said she didn't know. "It also doesn't make sense that he would leave us sleeping and then abandon us while he escaped and the space station was going to explode!"

Mars scowled. "That's why you can't trust him. He doesn't care about anyone."

Caddie looked thoughtful. "You'd be right, except it's strange that he happened to move us to a room right next to the shuttle. And that he had space suits all ready."

"That's HELGA," Mars said quickly. "She came through for us."

Caddie glanced curiously at HELGA, who was hibernating to save battery life. "So this is your new Martian friend?"

Mars smiled. "Yeah. It's a whole new world, Caddie."

They fell into silence, both lost in thought. Caddie tried not to be in Mars's head but as usual, it was impossible. She could feel his confusion, that he was having a hard time hating Oliver Pruitt, even though they were in this mess because of him.

"He's complicated," Caddie said.

Mars looked at her. "Are you doing it again? Being in my head?"

She shrugged. "I'm just saying, he's complicated. I don't think it's as simple as hating people. We have to work with each other."

"Caddie, Oliver Pruitt just tried to kill us. And now we're stranded in space thanks to him."

She nodded. "Maybe. Or maybe there's more going on." She looked out the small window, where they could see the vast expanse of space. And then something else. "What's that out there?"

Mars looked where she was pointing. "It's . . . a space shuttle. Hey, guys! It's Orion!"

Toothpick's ears pricked up. "Did you say space shuttle?" His eyes met Julia's. "Is there a way to talk to Orion?"

"Of course," Julia said immediately. She flipped the switches on the radio mic. "And I know where you're going with this. But it's harder than you think. Remember, there's no friction or gravity in space."

Toothpick shook his head. "With my plan, we won't need either."

∩

Orion was making his way toward the space station when he saw the whole thing detonate. The sound was epic, and the debris shooting out was like a brilliant and terrible show of dust, light, and flashing metal pieces. And then he was seized with panic. What was going on? Were they under attack? Was it the Martians? And what about his friends?

A few moments later, he received a ping from the Lifeboat.

"Come in, Orion. Do you read me?" It was Julia. She repeated herself. Then she added, "And by the way, the Pruitt Space Station is GONE if you didn't notice already."

They were alive!

Orion reached for the microphone switch. "I copy you, Julia," he said weakly. "Oh my god, stop scaring me already. What happened? Are you all OK? Daisy filled me in on the Martians. Over." She had filled him in, all right, not to mention the big reveal that Fang was Aurora (he always *knew* there was something off about her).

"We're OK. But we're in a bit of a jam," Julia said. "We've run out of fuel and we need you to help us out. Here's Randall—sorry, *Toothpick*, with the details. We found him on the space station along with Mars's other friends. Long story, don't ask."

"Greetings, Orion," came another voice though the speakers.

Orion knew immediately who Toothpick was. Mars had talked about him before. *Toothpick's a strange name*, Orion had commented. *Is he thin like a toothpick?* But that wasn't the reason. The nickname had nothing to do with the way Toothpick looked. Instead, Randall, aka Toothpick, had gone through a building frenzy when he was ten years old, making things out of toothpicks: London Bridge, the Eiffel Tower, the Statue of Liberty, the Space Needle. Hence the nickname.

"Hey, dude," Orion said now. "Cool name."

"Thank you. So Julia says you've only done it once in training. But that's OK. We'll guide you."

"Done what?" Orion asked cautiously.

Toothpick paused for a second before answering. "Tethering."

∩

Orion eased his space shuttle toward the Lifeboat, killing the engine as he approached. Julia was right. He'd tethered two spaceships together only once, and that was on a flight simulator during a learning module titled "How to Transfer Cargo Between Shuttles."

People weren't cargo, but they could be transferred just the same. You just had go out onto the exterior of the spacecraft, roll out the long satellite tether, and anchor it to the other ship. The tricky part was attaching the anchor on the other side, but Toothpick said his pet drone would handle that (pet drone?).

When Orion was ready, he braced himself as he went out the airlock. This was known as a spacewalk, when you went outside the space shuttle and tethered yourself with a cable. Astronauts did it all the time. Sometimes it was to repair something on the outside; sometimes it was to run experiments. Julia did it without batting an eye, but for Orion, who had done it only twice, it took several hours to work up the nerve so he wouldn't have "a moment" when he got out.

He didn't have the luxury of that now. Not when his friends were waiting in the stalled Lifeboat. As he sealed the airlock behind him, it was a good thing Orion was in a pressurized suit or he might just have stopped breathing right there. Holy mother of pearl! As always, the universe confronted him in all its glory. The endless stretch of infinity and beyond overwhelmed him. This was insane. Him out here. One cut of his tether and he would float away forever. And he knew what that meant. They had all been schooled in the awful consequences of getting separated from your shuttle. In fact, if he didn't successfully tether the Lifeboat and transfer his friends, they would experience the same fate. The Lifeboat would orbit Mars for a few hours until everyone on board ran out of oxygen. And that would be the end.

Orion shook himself. There wasn't time for what-ifs. He needed to secure his harness, double-check the jet pack, roll out the satellite tether, and wait for Droney.

Wait for Droney. Wait for Droney.

And there he was. A tiny drone was hovering over the Lifeboat, attaching the tether. In minutes, Droney moved deftly, maneuvering the end of the satellite tether and hooking it up to the Lifeboat. Done. Connected. *Easy peasy!* as Julia would say.

In his headpiece, he could hear cheering from the other end.

"Mission successful! Over!" Julia shouted in his ear.

Now that they were anchored, the hatch to the Lifeboat opened, and one by one, the passengers looped themselves to the satellite tether and moved single file toward Orion's shuttle. It was like a parade where no one was marching, just concentrating as hard as they could as they made the spacewalk to Orion's shuttle. None of them had ever done this. And JP, Caddie, and Toothpick hadn't even trained for space travel.

Orion breathed slowly to keep his heart from racing. He knew, and most of them did, too, how much their lives were in peril. At any moment, they could be hit by a zooming asteroid. A harness could snap.

Meanwhile, the minutes crawled by. The stars and planets watched.

One by one, the crew lowered themselves into Orion's shuttle. When HELGA dropped inside, holding Julia's rover, Orion closed the hatch and whispered a prayer of gratitude to the universe.

Once everyone was inside the airlock, they heaved a collective sigh of relief. There was now even room for hugging. "You did it!" Mars told Orion. "You really did!"

"Three cheers for Orion, Toothpick, and Droney!" Julia said.

"And Lost in London!" JP said. "Except she's not lost anymore. Or in London."

"If y'all don't mind me now, I'll be here resting my beating heart," Orion said.

"Perfect," Julia said. "In fact, we can head over to the Colony and rest up plenty there."

"Tell me we're not going back," Aurora said in dismay as Orion returned to the cockpit. "Someone wake me up from this nightmare."

Axel stepped forward and jiggled Aurora. She wrested herself away and glared at him. "Not literally!"

∩

As Orion was busy entering the coordinates for their return journey to Mars, Caddie's head began to throb inside her helmet. She tried to ignore it, but the pain was building. "Can I take this thing off now?" she asked, trying to keep her voice even. Maybe if she rubbed her temples, it would help. Though it never did.

"Sure, everyone take your helmets off for five," Orion said. "Put them back on when we're ready to descend. I'll give you the cue."

Meanwhile, Mars noticed something was off.

"Caddie, are you getting a headache?" he asked immediately. "No, just tired, that's all," Caddie said. She could feel him worrying. "Don't worry, Mars."

"Caddie's famous headaches," Aurora said tonelessly. She had observed their exchange. "You guys got really close. Must be hard being away from Mars, I bet," she said to Caddie. "I mean the person. Not the planet. You've never been there. If you did, you'd be crying now."

Caddie frowned. Aurora was looking at her with that stony, unreadable face of hers. How did Aurora always block Caddie out? At the same time, *she* was watching Caddie like a hawk. She never seemed to miss a thing. Would she guess what Caddie was thinking now?

Caddie turned her attention to the window overhead, trying to dismiss the worry mounting inside her. When they had been climbing across the tether from the Lifeboat to Orion's spaceship, she had been terrified of falling. In space. What could be more terrifying than that? Most of the time she moved with her eyes shut. She'd had reached one hand in front of the other, pulling herself forward, sensing her friends' movements to guide her. But now finally she could allow herself to appreciate the view. Her ideas of outer space had been built on movies like *Star Wars* and *2001: A Space Odyssey*, but seeing actual space was completely different. It felt like she was in perpetual darkness, a black inky tent punctuated by sharp pins of light. In the distance, a reddish shape came into view, like the wedge of an orange slice.

"Oh my god, that's Mars, isn't it?" JP called out, their eyes glued to the window.

Toothpick was struck into silence, too. He had studied

landing and colonization, watched video after video, and checked out books from the library, but nothing compared to this. "Where are we landing on Mars? Near Monument Crater?"

"Bingo," Orion said. "And flanked on the other side, Mount Olympus. Pretty awesome."

"Wait until we land," Mars said. "You won't believe it."

"Yeah, you'll lose all sense of reality," Aurora said bitterly.

"Mount Olympus?" Caddie repeated suddenly. Just saying those words was like squeezing her head in a vise. "Oww." She clutched her head.

Mars glanced at her quickly. "Caddie?"

She shook her head. She wasn't sure she could talk.

"Mount Olympus, Caddie," Toothpick said. "Mars's largest dormant volcano."

"Speaking of which, what I'd give for an Olympic burger," JP said. "I think my stomach was dormant until now."

"Olympic burger?" Julia asked. "Is that some American cuisine I'm unfamiliar with?"

"It's a mondo-size burger, named after Olympia, the capital of Washington," JP said. "You can buy it at the diner near my house. At least you could six months ago. Wait, we've been gone about six months, right? Not, like, six years or anything. Because *that* would be strange. They might not even be making Olympic burgers anymore."

"Oh my god, stop talking about burgers already," Aurora said.

"It's actually been about seven months," Mars explained.

"Activating decelerator," Orion called out. "Put on those helmets. Be sure you're strapped in."

Around them, people were sliding on their helmets and rebuckling their straps. Mars helped Caddie with hers, and then she felt his thoughts come at her: *I know something's wrong, Cads. You have to tell me.*

Caddie closed her eyes as her head throbbed and throbbed. She was grateful Mars understood, but what could either of them do right now? Were they going to crash? Were they going to die? Orion did seem to have everything under control. She could sense his expertise without even reading his mind.

Even so, there was something wrong, something frightening. Something to do with . . . Mount Olympus.

A harmless, dormant volcano.

Caddie blinked through the pain. "Keep us safe," she whispered to herself.

Just then, there was a rapid set of beeps from the cockpit.

"Is that Daisy?" Julia said from her seat. "Is she holding down the fort, Orion?"

He was about to respond when a message flashed on his screen.

"Daisy's such a goody-goody," Aurora said uncharitably.

"A do-gooder," Axel sneered.

"Why are you both hating on everyone?" JP asked. "I'm not getting good vibes from you, Aurora. We just rescued you, didn't we?"

"For the last time, nobody 'rescued' me!" Aurora said. "Don't you get it? We're returning to prison. Daisy's in charge, but in charge of what?"

"Let's start with your oxygen levels," Julia retorted. "And making sure people like you don't run the Colony to the ground." She noticed Orion, who was staring in alarm at the screen. "What's wrong, Orion? What happened to Daisy?"

20
BLAST

FROM THE PODCAST

(15) ▶ (30)

Hello? Hello?

In case you didn't notice, this isn't Oliver Pruitt.

This is Daisy Zheng, coming to you live from Colony
Command Central.

Soooo—how are things on Earth?

Out here, we have a little . . . volcano problem.

And by *little*, I mean a gigantic ash cloud

threatening to crush the entire Colony!

That's right—Mount Olympus has erupted!

That same dormant volcano that wasn't supposed to
erupt ever.

So how are we going to . . . you know . . . SURVIVE?

PS: If you're hearing this on Earth,

tell my parents . . . I love them.

633 Comments ⊗

andromeda   25 min ago
Omg Daisy!!

oreocookies   23 min ago
Sending good vibes daisy

neptunebaby   20 min ago
the planet Mars under attack #howitends

staryoda   15 min ago
It's a volcano #nature #howitends

galaxygenius   12 min ago
we have rain they have a volcano #howitends

zheng_family   9 min ago
Daisy, we love you. We are so proud to be your parents.

allie_j   1 min ago
I thought Oliver Pruitt was going to fix this

#moreofthesame #howitends

neptunebaby   30 sec ago
You out there mars patel? #howitends or #howitbegins

21

ASH CLOUD

There was only one good thing to say about the landing: at least they didn't crash.

This time, as Mars and the rest of the crew descended to the surface of the Red Planet, molten lava rained over them from the blood-red sky. Orion had to use his navigation coordinates and some old-fashioned intuition to cut through and land them on the tiny strip at the Colony, the plume of the ash cloud hanging dangerously a few miles away.

Flying past an erupting volcano was surreal. Actually, *the whole thing* was surreal. It was like an eerie déjà vu for Mars, who had seen footage of Mount Saint Helens exploding when his mom dragged him to the visitor center a few years ago. *This is part of your education*, she had lectured at him. They watched on film as the ash cloud from Saint Helens knocked down trees, killed off vegetation, and made the area a wasteland for years and years. *From the ashes, we grow,* his mom had said. She was right. The trees had come back. The wildlife had returned. But from these ashes on Mars, it wasn't clear what would grow or survive.

On the landing strip, the crew sprang to life as soon as the engine stopped.

"Please return your trays to their upright position," JP quipped, but was visibly shaken.

"Prepare to die," Aurora muttered. She wore a defiant look, but she was afraid, too, and was ready to disembark just as quickly as everyone else. Obviously, the best place to be after a volcano erupted was *not* in the space shuttle, but inside the Colony.

"Ready, everybody?" Orion asked, standing sentinel at the airlock of the space shuttle. "Check your helmets. Out we go. Three, two, one."

When they got to the tunnels, chaos had erupted inside the Colony. Kids were scattered everywhere in panic. At least a dozen were crying in the dining hall. Orion tried to round up as many as he could and made them go down to the emergency shelter on Sublevel 3. Near the elevators, he shooed away a few thrill seekers taking selfies in front of the glass dome, presumably waiting for the ash cloud to come.

"Y'all crazy?' he scolded them and sent them down to the shelter as well.

"Is that all of them?" JP asked breathlessly as they followed Orion to the security wing.

Orion shook his head grimly. "These are just the kids I found now," he said. "But there have to be more wandering around. Daisy would know."

A few moments later, Orion slammed the door open to the control room—where they found Daisy shaking over the podcast equipment. Her eyeliner had run, and her hair was a hot mess.

"Daisy, enough with the broadcast," Orion said, exasperated as he pulled off his helmet.

Daisy hastily clicked off the microphone. "Orion! That was such a stellar landing and . . . and . . . I'm sorry. I'm trying to stay positive, but, like, honestly, we just had a volcano explode, and now we have earthquakes—I mean marsquakes—and there's a gigantic ash cloud heading our way. Hard to find a silver lining with that." Her eyes flickered to Mars and Caddie, who were pulling off their helmets, too.

Caddie stepped forward. "Hi," she said to Daisy. "I'm Caddie. Though I guess this isn't the best of circumstances to meet."

"Hi, Caddie," Daisy said weakly. "Welcome to the experience of a lifetime at the Mars Colony and . . ." Her lower lip quivered.

Orion and Mars went to look at the wall monitors to

assess the damage. Were kids trapped in the tunnels? Were the elevators working? Was the power on in the greenhouse and loading docks? So far, none of the images were coming through. Orion turned to talk to HELGA while Mars tried reloading the video images but it was no use. All the surveillance cameras had stopped working, and much of the Colony server appeared to be down.

Meanwhile Orion continued talking to HELGA. "How much of the evacuation do you think is completed?"

"Can HELGA tell you?" Caddie asked him curiously.

"She just she told me that there were ways for her to connect to our system," Orion said. "I'm not sure, but I think she's *learning* stuff she wasn't programmed to do."

"That's amazing," Caddie said. She paused as if considering her words. "Sorry, HELGA," she said to the robot. "I mean, *you're* amazing."

"Thank you, Caddie," HELGA said. "I am surprising myself, too. Technically, I have only restricted access to the Ad Astra server here. But as Julia says, I 'hacked the hack.' I have discovered a back door to the internal bot system, which is running despite most of the server being down."

"Terrific," Orion said. "What did you find?"

"According to bot data, fifty-two percent of the Colony is in the emergency shelter."

"So half the kids are still out there." Caddie turned to Mars. "Didn't you say there's, like, four hundred Colonists? That means about two hundred kids are still unaccounted for."

"Man!" Mars clearly didn't like where this was going.

"More missing kids," Caddie said softly. Orion was looking agitated, too. He was the one who'd brought everyone on the shuttle from the space station. He knew their shiny faces. He'd fielded their questions about what life was like at the Colony. He knew the names of everyone still missing.

"Daisy, where are the rest of the kids?" he demanded.

"I don't know!" she burst out. "The sensors are down. Most of the tunnels to the surface have collapsed. The other tunnels are losing air. The kids could be *anywhere*." Her voice grew more and more despondent. "I used to know where everyone was. It was my job. Now I don't know *anything*!" Daisy's shoulders heaved and she crumpled.

Caddie stepped forward, taking care not to knock over the towering stack of data printouts on the floor. "It's OK," she said gently. She put her arm around Daisy, gently patting the once-sparkly hair that now drooped in sorry ringlets around Daisy's shoulders. "We're going find those kids. Don't worry."

Daisy nodded and pretended to scratch her nose even though she was really trying stop herself from crying.

Orion took a breath. "Listen, we need to get everyone down to the emergency shelter. OK? Let's put our heads together and find a way."

At this Mars, looked up. "What about Aurora?"

Daisy was surprised. "I totally forgot. Where is she—and the rest of the crew?"

"Julia and Toothpick went straight to the weather tower," Caddie said. "They wanted to follow up on the ash cloud." She fell silent. She knew the next part was going to make Mars mad, *again*.

"Why don't you tell her, Caddie?" Mars's voice was sharp. "Orion didn't think we could trust them, Daisy, so he had Aurora and Axel locked up in the service room on Sublevel 2. JP's watching them. I *knew* it was a bad idea."

"My god, stop worrying about her, Fly!" Orion said, irritated. "I get it. You hate what I did. But they commandeered the Lifeboat, and now we don't have that shuttle anymore. I don't care if it was because the space station blew up. If they'd stayed put in the first place, we'd have one more shuttle with us. Anyway, Aurora and Axel are just as safe as everybody else. You got to start thinking about the rest of the kids. The ones above ground or trapped in the tunnels. *They're* the ones in danger." He studied the monitors on the wall. "Daisy, can you show us *any* of the tunnel views?"

Daisy typed furiously on the keyboard. "The cameras still aren't working," she said sadly. "Oh no. Now the secondary tunnels are losing air, too!"

"Fine, then. We'll start with the main tunnels," Orion said. "First, let's check in with Julia and Toothpick."

Orion saw that the signal on his IP phone seemed to be working, so he called the weather tower. "Hey Julia, do you read me? What's the status of the volcano from up there? Over."

A boy's voice answered. "This is Toothpick," he said. "We read you. We can see the ash cloud from the volcano. In the last thirty minutes, it's worsened. It's now coming toward the Colony. It's coming fast. Think tornado meets Miami Beach."

"Are you sure, Pick?" Mars asked.

"Yes, Mars. I'm not going to lie to you. We predict total havoc and destruction."

Julia cut in. "Toothpick is right. When the ash cloud reaches us, it will bring down every structure above ground. I repeat. It will bring down everything—the green-house, the domes, the cafeteria, all of it. Over."

"There is no protocol for this situation," Daisy cried. "There is no protocol."

"Then we need to find one," Mars said. "We can't let that ash cloud get to us."

"How much time do we have?" Caddie asked, her face pale.

"Maybe twenty minutes," Julia said gravely. "Depending on the wind. Visibility up here is near zero."

"Hang tight," Orion said soberly. "You guys need to fig-ure out a way to slow that ash down, OK? Two heads are better than one. Keep your helmets on just in case. Over and out."

After the call, Orion, Caddie, Mars, and Daisy stood silently in the control room looking at the empty monitor screens.

"Maybe it isn't as bad as you think," Caddie ventured.

"Or it's worse," Daisy said. "Our sensors are down, we're cut off from the kids, and a monster ash cloud is on its way to wipe us out. It's like we're caught in a web, but we don't know which direction the spider is coming from. We don't even know if it's a spider or a bat or . . ."

"Thanks for the analogy, Daisy," Mars interrupted. "But listen, maybe *we* don't have a full picture, but what about Pruitt Prep? Don't they get satellite images of the Colony?"

"Mars is correct," HELGA announced. "I can make an IP call to Pruitt Prep for you."

"Awesome, HELGA," Orion said. "Call away."

HELGA did that thing again with her metal lips, bending them into a U as she put through the call. Around them, the walls of the control room shook violently.

"Just aftershocks from the volcano," Orion said. "No worries, y'all."

Caddie squeezed Daisy's hand.

There was static on the overhead speakers, and then a voice came through.

"This is Pruitt Prep Mission Control Earth, Jonas

Hopkins speaking. Come in, Mars Colony Control."

"Jonas!" Mars exclaimed. It was their old friend from Port Elizabeth, who had been one of the first kids to disappear. "Is that you?"

"It's so great to hear your voice!" Caddie chimed in. "Last time we saw you, you were in the infirmary!"

Jonas was equally surprised. "Mars! Caddie! Hey, guys. Whoa—you're all there! Yeah, my leg's all healed!" he said. He was the first one to get injured at Pruitt Prep, when they were trying to stage an escape. But that was before anyone knew Mars and his friends were destined for space. "We were told about the sleep pods. Wild stuff! And—"

"Listen guys, can you cut the school reunion?" Orion said. "Jonas, can you tell us more about the eruption? How bad is it? Over."

"Roger," Jonas said. "That volcano is epic. You got a plume of fifty kilometers, gale-force winds, and an ash cloud that's moving fast. We've been running numbers, and listen to this. That was no ordinary eruption. Not how the top blew off like that. It was an explosion. That's the only thing that could have triggered it."

"An explosion?" Orion asked slowly. "You mean, like . . . a bomb?"

Caddie could feel Daisy shivering next to her.

"That's exactly what I'm saying," Jonas said. "In fact—"

There was a beep and Jonas's voice cut off.

"Connection lost, I'm afraid," HELGA said. "Shall I try reconnecting?"

Orion shook his head. "I heard enough," he said quietly. "I don't believe it. It can't be."

"Believe what?" Mars asked.

Meanwhile, Caddie frowned as Orion's thoughts filtered in.

"Orion," she said suddenly. "You mean a *person* set off the eruption?"

By now Orion had reached the door.

"Daisy, Caddie, Mars," he said urgently. "It's your job to get one hundred percent of the kids to the emergency shelter. No one gets left behind. I gotta go take care of something I should have done already."

"Wait, Orion," Mars called out after him. "Where are you going?"

"*Not* to the stars," Orion declared before he stormed out.

22
HOLDING DOWN THE FORT

When Julia was younger, her favorite book series was I Survived, with pictures of major disasters that had struck around the world. Her favorite one was on Pompeii, the ancient Roman city covered by molten rock and ash when Mount Vesuvius erupted. For Julia, natural disasters had never been frightening, but a chance to learn how *she* would handle them if the time came. But she never expected that time would be *now*. For a moment, all she and Toothpick could do was gape at the mammoth ash cloud that was making its way toward the Colony as the wind outside the tower howled.

Then she snapped out of it.

"Toothpick, stop staring."

"The ash cloud is going to smother the Colony and everything above the surface," he said.

Next to him, Droney chittered. "Smothering will commence with this weather tower."

"Droney's right," Toothpick said.

"Well, tell your drone to put a sock in it," Julia said. "I was given an assignment, and I will NOT abandon my post. Orion is depending on us to solve this volcanic ash problem. And that's what I'm going to do."

"I was given the same assignment," Toothpick said. "And I should tell you that the probability of solving this problem in time is close to zero."

"In life there are always risks," Julia said. It had been years since she had walked unaided. The rover was a brilliant transport device that moved with her body, that kept her safe and upright and mobile. But even before the rover, she had discovered ways to be fully engaged with the world. She didn't need to be able-bodied to be a scientist or to travel to Mars. In fact, her disability gave her a different way of looking at the world. All her life, she had figured things out by herself in London. Now she would need to figure things out here. This ash cloud—it was a setback, but maybe it simply required a new way of solving the problem.

Still, just because she wanted to face this problem head-on didn't mean everyone should. "That's why you need to leave the weather tower, Toothpick. One person can hold down the fort. And . . . I can be that person."

"I'm not going anywhere, Julia," he said. "Not if the probability is greater than zero."

"But I thought . . ."

"I'm not afraid of risks. I came to Mars, didn't I?"

"Yes. As did I."

"If you stay, I stay," he said simply.

He said it with so much conviction, Julia fell silent in surprise.

She looked more closely at him. Toothpick. What an odd name for this boy. He was thin and his glasses sometimes slid down his nose, but he was nothing like a toothpick. He was strong, resourceful, and now he just said that he was going to see this thing through with her.

When Julia saw him, it was like looking at herself.

∩

Mars made HELGA try to connect with Pruitt Prep Mission Control again.

"Pruitt Prep, come in," Mars said into the speaker.

"We are unable to make a connection," HELGA said. "There is no point speaking into a microphone that isn't heard."

"I have to do something," Mars said. He frowned. "I'm going to step outside and see if my IP phone works there. The signal seems to come and go."

"Stay nearby, Mars," Caddie said. "In case Jonas contacts us again."

"I'll be back in five. HELGA, please keep trying to connect to Pruitt Prep."

"My pleasure," HELGA said.

Meanwhile, Daisy was growing more desperate.

"We're all going to die!" she moaned after Mars had gone.

"Daisy, please calm down," Caddie said.

"I really messed up," she said tearfully. "It's really bad because I know everyone thinks I'm a picture of togetherness."

"Um," Caddie said. So far, all she was seeing were streaks of blue eyeliner running down Daisy's face. Even so, Caddie *could* picture a different Daisy in her head, an ultraconfident girl who used color-coded sheets to inspect tunnels, maintain schedules, and track students. Maybe it was a hunch or a keen intuition, but Caddie was sure that this other Daisy had existed before, a person on top of her game, who knew where everyone was and what they were doing. There had to be a way to get *that* Daisy back.

"You were great welcoming me to the Colony just a few minutes ago," Caddie tried.

"That was *terrible*," sobbed Daisy, wilting to the floor. "And I didn't even give you the whole welcome speech."

Caddie sighed. If only there were some magical way to get the system up and running again. She certainly didn't know anything about computers. She couldn't hack her way into anything. Her power was in understanding others. Now she was alone with a robot and a weeping girl. How would her power of empathy help her now?

The door opened—Mars again.

"No luck with the phone," he said. "Did Jonas call again?"

"Negative," HELGA said.

Mars looked at Daisy on the floor. "How is she?"

"The same," Caddie said.

"I was Mr. Pruitt's pride and joy," Daisy wept. "Now everyone's *lost*, and I don't know how to find them!"

"I can find them!" Caddie suddenly said.

Daisy paused in her crying. "You? How can you?"

Mars was nodding. "That's right. Caddie can do it! Why didn't we think of that before?"

"I can hear them in my head if I'm close enough. But I don't know my way around here."

"But Daisy does," Mars said.

Daisy dried her eyes. "I know all the tunnels and passageways," she said slowly.

"If we work together, we can find everybody and bring them to the shelter," Caddie said. "Do you think you can help me?"

Daisy got up from the floor. "Yes. I can." It was the first time she'd sounded calm in hours. "We can do it together."

"I'll stay here with HELGA and try to get back in touch

with Jonas," Mars said. "Be careful, Caddie. It's getting really dark out there."

"You, too, Mars. Be safe," Caddie said. "Come on Daisy. I know we can do it."

Now that she had a plan, Daisy's breathing had slowed down to almost normal. "Let's go," she said.

23

WIND

For a while, Mars thought he'd been happier thinking his friends were safe on Earth and spared the journey of coming to Mars—along with the dangers of volcanic eruptions, exploding space stations, missing kids, and Oliver Pruitt being MIA. But the truth was he was so relieved they were here. Toothpick had joined Julia in the weather tower, JP was keeping an eye on Aurora, and Caddie was so quietly confident, everyone felt instantly better around her.

As Mars waited in the control room, he asked HELGA to put in a call to the weather tower. This time the signal seemed to work.

"Julia, Toothpick, do you read me? Can you give me an update on the ash cloud?"

"Roger, Mars," Toothpick said. "Still bad."

"If we don't stop it, ALL the structures aboveground will be wiped out," Julia said.

Mars stopped, suddenly comprehending. "But *you're* in the weather tower, Julia," he sputtered. "That's aboveground, too."

Until now, Mars hadn't realized the implication of the situation.

"Toothpick and me," Julia corrected him. "And his droney friend."

"Then both of you have to get out of there," Mars said desperately. "Come back inside."

"Negative on that, Mars," Toothpick said.

"Imminent ash cloud," HELGA said. "They have ten minutes before the ash cloud reaches the weather tower, based on outside bot calculations."

"Toothpick! Julia! Come *on*."

"Mars, we're not going to leave until we find a way to stop the ash cloud," Julia said. "Aren't there still kids up near the surface?"

For a moment, Mars had no answer. Of course there were kids near the surface. But did that mean Toothpick and Julia had to risk their lives? "Caddie is finding them now," he said.

"It will still take time," Toothpick said. "We have to stay here, Mars." He continued over Mars's protests. "We're the ones who have to find a solution. Just tell Caddie to hurry. Power is going down. Nuclear power out. Solar power out. Wind power will go out next."

"Wind power?" Mars repeated.

"Yeah. You know, those ginormous windmills."

Toothpick was talking about the four windmills positioned at the cliffs right between the Colony and the volcanic range, where they could harness the most wind as it blew over the valley. The first day Mars had come to the Colony, he had seen them pinwheeling in the distance. Now hearing Pick talking about them gave Mars a daring idea. But would it work?

He turned quickly to HELGA. "How much power do those windmills give to the Colony?"

"About twenty-five percent of the Colony's power," HELGA said. "Think big light switch."

"What are you getting at, Mars?" asked Toothpick, who could hear them talking.

"Pick, remember in third grade, Mrs. Lutz and her perfume? How it was really strong and made you want to puke?"

"Mrs. Lutz and her perfume?" Julia asked skeptically. "Where are you going with this?"

"Yes," Toothpick said over Julia. "I remember. I was allergic to that scent."

"Gardenia," Mars said. "Right?"

"Affirmative. And she made me sit in the front row. The perfume was so strong I thought I would faint."

"That's when I thought up the desk fan idea."

"Right. You rigged it so I could switch it on remote. Every time she walked by, I turned on the fan, and poof—the perfume smell was blown away."

"Guys, I fail to see how this is relevant," Julia said.

"Is there any way to do the same thing?" Mars asked quickly. "Can we use the windmills like gigantic fans and blow away the ash?"

"So we're taking energy from the Colony and feeding it to windmills?" Toothpick asked.

There was a silence. For a moment Mars was afraid the connection was cut.

"Mars . . . that is pure brilliance," Julia said. "Forgive me, but I think I have to marry you now."

"Uh, thanks?" Mars said, flushing. "So can you guys do it? Can you reverse the windmills?"

"Absolutely," Julia said, "Right, Pick?"

"Affirmative. We will siphon off the energy from every other place in the Colony and send it to the windmills. If we have enough juice, we can blow away the ash clouds."

Mars cheered and grinned at HELGA, who did her upward-U smile.

"Hurrah," HELGA said, and gave Mars a high five. She was really starting to grow on him.

"OK, let's hope it works, guys," he said. "If it does, I'll tell Caddie so she knows. Or maybe she can read my mind or something."

"Mind reading," HELGA said. "That is not in my programming language."

"Of course not," Mars said. "It's just something Caddie does. It's a Caddie thing."

"We'll keep you posted on Operation Windmill," Julia said.

"It should give Caddie and Daisy enough time to find everyone and bring them to the emergency shelters," Toothpick said. "If it works, that is."

"It will," Mars said immediately, even though he had no idea whether it would. His eyes met HELGA's. "Over and out."

After they hung up, HELGA spoke. "My facial-expression recognition software informs me that you just lied. Why did you do that, Mars?"

"I didn't lie!"

"You misspoke," HELGA said. "You do not know that Operation Windmill will work. In fact, the possibility of its success is remote. Is this called being a friend?"

"I was being positive," Mars said. "That's what friends do. You hope it all works out and the universe comes through for you." Just saying that made Mars's heart lift for the first time that day. Now they just had to wait and see if the plan would work.

"You and my training software have different notions of the universe," HELGA said.

24
END OF THE WORLD

The first set of kids that Caddie and Daisy found were in the cafeteria: a boy and identical twin girls. Robert had been hungry, so Gia and Loretta said they would go to the cafeteria with him to get milkshakes. That was before the volcano blew. By the time Caddie and Daisy found them, all three kids were in tears.

"I miss my mama," Gia said. "I don't want to die on Mars."

Caddie put her arms around Gia while Daisy checked the name tags on all three.

"We're taking you to the stairwell," Daisy said. "Don't use the elevators. When you get to the stairs, it's three flights down, and you're in the emergency shelter."

"Are there milkshakes down there?" Loretta asked, drying her eyes.

"Of course," Daisy lied.

The three kids went without hesitation.

Jimmy in Tunnel C threw a fit. Caddie had to play a mind game to get him to go down the stairwell. "I know who your best friend in first grade was," she told him. "He stole your stuffed animal, Grumpus, and never gave it back."

Jimmy was so shocked that he stopped midhowl and walked wordlessly down the staircase.

As they went from place to place, they found groups of friends, straggling loners, funny kids, angry kids, and some who wouldn't believe anything unless they saw it for themselves. In the end, Caddie and Daisy got all of them down the stairs to the emergency shelters. Daisy kept tabs: four hundred kids in the shelter, twenty left to go. Caddie found herself drawn to each one, even the ones who were normally troublemakers. Something about them moved her, their soulful fear of what would happen next.

Daisy was holding up, too. She wasn't the chirpy girl she'd been before, but all the things Daisy knew—the layout of the Colony, the names and faces—the *facts* had come back.

"This way," Daisy directed. "No, turn there. Go down that way. Three doors to right. Then the stairs. Be careful about the third step from the bottom. It's a steep one."

She didn't need a clipboard. The checklist was in her head. The age eights were accounted for. So were the age nines. Three of the age tens were missing. And so on.

They were on their way to the surface when, without warning, the lights went out.

At first, Daisy's thoughts came scattering through Caddie's head like flashes of lightning: *This is it. This is the end. The tens, the elevens—there's still so many to go!*

Caddie braced for the meltdown. But then surprisingly Daisy just turned on the light on her IP phone. It wasn't super-bright, but it was enough to light the way.

"We can still see," she said. "And you can, too, right? In your mind, that is."

Caddie checked around them. "The greenhouse. Three people. How do we get there?"

"The shortest way is through the greenhouse tunnel behind us," Daisy said. "But it's one of the tunnels that's lost oxygen."

"I knew I should have kept my helmet," Caddie said ruefully. Everyone else from the shuttle flight had held onto theirs, but Caddie had dumped hers in the control room because of her headache.

"I don't have my helmet, either," Daisy said. "I guess we could stick to the main tunnels. But they take twice as long to go through and they might lose oxygen, too. Also, we're running out of time!"

Caddie could feel Daisy's fear surfacing again. If she had another panic attack, they were finished. "Let's go through the small tunnel," Caddie said quickly. "We'll just . . . hold our breath and run."

"Run," Daisy repeated, turning the word over in her mind. "OK, we can do that."

"We can," Caddie said. She and Daisy took a deep breath and ran.

In the weather tower, Julia and Toothpick were in a frenzy to get everything shut down.

"Charging station off—that gives us ten percent," Toothpick said. "Shutting down cafeteria. Eight percent."

"Laundry, another ten," Julia reported.

Back and forth they went, looking for places to siphon off precious energy to send to the windmills.

"The windmills have never operated at this capacity before," Julia said. "Or at that speed."

"It will have to work," Toothpick said simply. "We don't have any choice."

Outside, the wind howled more fiercely than ever. Without warning, the tower shuddered violently, shaking from side to side.

"What on earth?" Julia exclaimed. She went to the window to see what had happened. "I don't believe it. It's raining rocks."

Toothpick looked up. "Droney, can it do that on Mars?"

Droney whirred and clicked. "Julia is reporting the occurrence of molten rock ejected from the volcano known as lava bombs."

"Oh," Toothpick said. "Lava bombs. I know those. They did a whole show about them on *Ancient Aliens*."

"Well, those lava bombs are going to bring down the weather tower," Julia said. "We have to hurry."

"We are hurrying," Toothpick said. "We can't hurry more."

The tower shook violently again as pieces of ceiling came down.

"Tell that to the lava bombs," Julia said. "Greenhouse, five percent."

"Gymnasium, seven." Toothpick paused to add it up. "I think that's all we have."

"Time to send," Julia said. She could hear the wind and volcanic rocks doing their awful thing outside. It really did feel like the end of the world. But what world was that? The one where she was from, where she had left her parents, and her classmates (who'd never understood her that much anyway)? Or the one she had come to, this strange, beautiful, deadly planet that didn't seem to want anyone to succeed, but beckoned to her anyway. How many hours, how many minutes did they have left? "Toothpick, if this doesn't work," she said softly, "just so you know, it's been an honor."

"Likewise," Toothpick said. "We'll remember this, right?"

"Always. And someday, we'll tell our kids this story. I mean, not *our* kids, like our kids together. I mean our own set of kids. Oh dear. Well, you know what I mean."

"Yes, because I'm with Epica," Toothpick said. "Our kids separately."

"Epica's the one who did that heroic thing," Julia said, "with her shoes." She remembered the incident on the boat, where Toothpick's girlfriend had thrown her wedges at an oncoming attacker. "I saw that from the drone."

"The one and only," Toothpick said.

They both put on their helmets as Toothpick made an IP call to Mars.

"We're ready," he said.

"Ready here, too," Mars said. "Send the power. Over."

"Roger," Toothpick said. "Sending all power to the fans."

"And all good thoughts," Julia said through the glass visor of her helmet.

"And all good thoughts," Toothpick said. "Count for us, Droney."

Droney obliged. "Countdown T minus fifteen, T minus fourteen . . ."

They watched from the windows of the weather tower.

"It's not enough," Julia whispered. "Look, the ash cloud is still gaining." She scoured her brain for another place, then looked up. "Kill the lights. Shutting down weather tower, ten percent. Hit it, Toothpick."

There was a final surge.

"I can't see a thing from here," Mars said. "You have to tell me."

"It's . . . it's . . ." Toothpick paused. "It's working. It's working!"

"The windmills are holding off the ash cloud!" Julia said. "Mars, your idea worked!"

"But you're the ones who did it!" Mars said. "You're the ones who saved us!"

"Tell Caddie and Daisy to hurry," Julia said. "Get everyone to safety. We'll stay here as long as we can. The windmills won't hold off the cloud forever." She and Toothpick watched the ash cloud in the distance, a big monster blob of destruction. "Not yet," she told the ash cloud. "Not yet."

In the control room, Mars heaved a sigh of relief.

"See, HELGA?" he said. "The universe came through!"

"Your friends had less than a five percent probability of averting the ash cloud," HELGA said. "Your friends beat the odds. That is what is known as a miracle."

"I know!" Mars said. "Humans do it all the time."

The door opened.

"Whoa, it sure looks like the end of the world here."

"JP! You're here!" Mars exclaimed. "What about Aurora and Axel? Aren't you guarding them?"

JP took off their helmet. "Hey, Mars, nice to see you, too. Just so you know, I'm freezing my tush off." In the service room where Aurora and Axel were locked up, the lights had gone off and so had the heating. JP had come up to investigate.

"The power's out because Toothpick and Julia are grabbing it from wherever they can," Mars said. He filled JP in on Operation Windmill. "It will hold off the ash, but not forever. Caddie and Daisy are trying to find everyone who's missing and get them down to the shelters."

"Um . . . speaking of missing, add Aurora and Axel to the list because . . ." JP swallowed. "I kinda let them out."

"You did what?" Mars jumped up from his seat.

"I thought you'd be happy, Mars! You didn't like what Orion did. Neither did I. Remember, Aurora is our friend. She's the reason we're here, isn't she?"

"Yeah, JP, but the volcano . . ."

"Look, Mars," JP said. "I'm sorry. We'll find them. I mean, how far could they have gone?"

"The lava tubes extend in miles in all directions," HELGA stated. "It might be a miracle if they got very far. But we have ascertained that miracles do happen."

"Thanks, sunshine," JP said.

"This is terrible," Mars said. "She's not the same person since she got here, JP. She does random things without any warning or thinking it through."

"Uh, that sounds *exactly* like Aurora," JP said.

Mars put on his helmet. "I need to find her. It's not safe out there."

JP let out a breath. "How long can you keep doing this? Aurora can take care of herself."

"Well, so can I," Mars said. "I'll be back as soon as I can. You stay here. And JP, don't *do* anything, OK?"

JP nodded. "Roger. I'm the star of doing nothing."

∩

After Mars had left, JP rested their helmet on the counter and settled back in one of the console chairs. "So HELGA, what's it like to be a robot?"

"I beg your pardon?" asked HELGA pleasantly. "Are you inquiring about the design of my circuits? Or the materials used? I am a prototype, but there will be more made of me in the future."

"That's wild!" JP said. "But no, I don't mean how were you made. I mean, what's it like? Do you enjoy being a robot?"

"Robots do not experience enjoyment when it comes to existential considerations. Do you enjoy being a human being?"

"Do I . . . what?" JP laughed. "OK, fine. Yeah, I do enjoy being me. I'd enjoy me a lot more if I had a tuna sandwich. But I guess we have bigger problems right now."

"I'm afraid so," HELGA said. "You must put aside the

immediate needs of your human body. You must think about the other human beings in the Colony. Even Aurora Gershowitz, who so far has not displayed compassion or other adaptive qualities."

"Yeesh, don't get me started on that girl," JP said. They paused. "Speaking of which, how come you're a girl robot? Everyone is using 'she' with you."

"That was the pronoun assigned to me," HELGA said. "What about you?"

"I use they."

"Because you chose differently at birth?"

"Because I'm not one or the other." JP thought for a moment. "And I don't see why a robot has to be one or the other."

"I am in concurrence," HELGA said. "I believe my settings can be changed."

"Like with a button?" JP asked.

"No. I am an adaptive robot. I will now answer to they."

"Wow," JP said. "That's cool."

HELGA turned their mouth up in a U smile. "Cool," they said.

By now, JP had noticed a red light flashing on the wall next to the monitors. "Hey HELGA, what does that red light mean? Am I supposed to do something? Even if Mars said *not* to?"

"I am consulting the emergency manual downloaded

into my system," HELGA said. "The flashing light is part of the emergency warning system."

"And?" JP prompted. "You're killing me, sunshine."

"I certainly am not. And I'm not an independent source of energy, either."

"It's an expression, HELGA! Tell me now!"

"According to that flashing light, the weather tower is emitting a distress signal."

"Oh my god. Isn't that where Toothpick and Julia are?"

"Yes," HELGA said. "JP, your friends are in grave danger."

25

A PROMISE IS A PROMISE

Aurora was sick of everyone. First Orion locked her and Axel up in the service room like they were animals. (Then Axel did kind of act like an animal when he howled and kicked at the door, but give him some slack—he was tired of being holed up). Thank god JP had let them out.

As Aurora and Axel were sauntering along one of the tunnels up on Ground Level, they ran into a group of kids heading down to the emergency shelters.

"Why are you going to Sublevel Three?" Aurora asked, surprised. "We were just there. All the power's gone." Aurora had never seen so many Colonists in one place before. It was like a parade, except they were all huddled together and looked scared.

"The volcano erupted," said one of them, a girl named Gish. Aurora knew her. They had been in the greenhouse together that day when the Martians came and got her.

"We know," Aurora said. "But it's miles away. We missed it, didn't we?"

"Yeah, Mount Olympus isn't our problem," Axel said.

"That's not what we were told," Gish said. "The ash cloud is coming. That's why we're evacuating as far down as we can go. Daisy told us to go to the emergency shelter. They have a generator set up there."

"Little Daisy," Aurora said.

Gish watched Axel spray-painting his name on the tunnel wall. He had found the spray paint stored in the service room and brought it along with him.

"You should come, too, Aurora," Gish said, "you and Axel. It's not safe in the upper levels. The ash cloud is going to destroy everything." A murmur of fear ran through the huddle of Colonists. "Don't worry, guys," Gish told them. "It's safe in the emergency shelters. Daisy said so."

For the first time what Gish said had started to register with Aurora.

"Does that mean the lava tubes aren't safe either?" she asked, worried.

"I don't know," Gish said. "I gotta go, Aurora. But it was nice seeing you."

"Yeah, we'll catch up later, OK?" Aurora said gruffly.

After Gish and the rest of the group had gone, Aurora turned to Axel. "Did you hear that? The lava tubes probably aren't safe. Most of them are near the surface. What if the tops of them cave in? There could be quakes and tremors."

Axel was snickering as he painted flames at the end of his name. "Ha, ha—check out this tag. I'm painting my name all over Pruitt's beautiful tunnel. Take that, sucker!"

"Axel, did you hear a word I said?"

"Yeah, don't worry, Aurora. We're safe." Axel did a jump in the air and landed, laughing. "Whee! Watch me now!"

"You call this safe? What about the Martian kids still in the lava tubes? Who's taking them to the shelter? Who's going to stop the ash cloud and tremors from hurting them?"

Axel stopped laughing. "Hmm. I guess I'm not sure."

"We have to bring them back to the Colony," Aurora said. "We have to go to the tubes and get them."

"But the entry is sealed," he said. "You saw what they did. They built an airlock."

"Right," Aurora said. "But it can still be opened from this side. That means you go, Axel, and I'll stay. I'll wait at the airlock and let you all in."

"You'll stay?" Axel asked doubtfully. "I don't want to get stuck in the tubes either."

"You need to save them, and I need you guys." Aurora paused. "For what I've planned next."

"What you've planned . . . are you plotting again? 'Cause I know that look. It's your Fang look."

Aurora gave a small smile. The sudden worry she had

felt with Gish had given way to something else: an opportunity staring her in the eye.

"Let's just say Mars isn't the only one with plans," she said. She was remembering H. G. Wells Middle School, where distraction was key when it came to disrupting the teachers and the principal. Maybe she could use that idea to her advantage now. "If we're going to get out of this place alive, Axel, we need to take control. They will never see us coming."

"Ha, ha," Axel said in delight. "Maybe *you're* the disaster they should all be worried about."

🎧

"I think we've got some breathing room," Toothpick said. "Look at the ash cloud. It hasn't moved at all."

Julia was peering at the sky. "Maybe, but I don't like the look of those lava bombs that have been falling down around us. It seems to be getting worse. We have to go."

"Go? What do you mean?"

"I mean like *go*," Julia said. "We've done all we can. The windmills are going to keep going whether we're here or not. We better leave before the lava bombs destroy the whole tower."

"But Mars is counting on us to stay," Toothpick said.

"No, he's counting on us to *live*," Julia said. "Come on, before—"

But before she could finish her sentence, there was a terrible crumbling sound.

The ceiling came crashing down around them.

"Bollocks!" Julia exclaimed. In the cloud of debris, she felt her helmet, glad that they had both put them on. The Martian air was quickly leaking into the tower. She rolled over to look at Toothpick, who was lying inert beneath a pile of rubble. "Oh my word, Toothpick! You're bleeding!"

Toothpick tried to stir, but it was useless. He was pinned down by a large piece of ceiling.

"It's just a flesh wound," he said weakly through his helmet. "That's a line from a movie."

"Toothpick! This is no time for movie trivia. We have to get you out of here." She tried making a call on her IP phone. "It's not working," she said grimly. "I can't get a signal anymore."

"No problemo," Toothpick said. "I'll just float off and . . ."

"Toothpick, hang on. Don't float off. You have to stay awake."

On the one remaining wall, Julia spotted an emergency button. Would that work? Would the control room hear her call for help? She slowly moved to an upright position, balancing on her rover, which was miraculously still working in spite of the ceiling caving in on her. She maneuvered herself gingerly around the rubble to the wall and gave the button a hard push, then another and another for good measure.

"Julia, something tells me this is mucho bad," Toothpick murmured.

"Mucho bad?" Julia asked. "You must be in trouble if that's your best attempt at Spanish."

"Really, you gotta go, Julia," Toothpick said. "I can . . . hold down the port."

"That's *fort*," Julia corrected. "Hold down the fort. And I don't think so. You stay, I stay."

Toothpick was losing blood, and he was losing clarity. Julia moved back to him and checked his helmet—no visible cracks. That was good. Over their heads, it was already dark. Temperatures had plummeted. Luckily they were both wearing space suits, which kept them warm, but how long could they handle the cold Martian night? Julia also knew that the oxygen in their suits would run out. Plus, her rover would need charging soon. She had to find a way to get Toothpick back inside the Colony while her rover still worked. After that? Well, she wasn't going to worry about that yet. For right now, she used a plastic bag and several rubber bands to stanch the bleeding from his leg. It wasn't professional, but it worked.

"At least the wind has shifted," she said. "We're not in danger of getting smothered by an ash cloud. Now we just have the usual things to look out for: getting brained by a lava bomb, being attacked by the Martians, or dying of hypothermia. Not bad. Like a trip to the beach."

"I know you're joking," Toothpick said, talking with effort. "Because that's how . . . you deal with being scared. It's your . . . defense mechanism."

"You should rest, Toothpick. Don't talk."

"Julia . . . are you sorry you came to Mars?"

"Not for a second," she said. "Whatever happens, I was here. Really here."

"Yeah," Toothpick said. "Me too. We all were."

Just then, the mangled door to the weather tower pushed forward, and two figures burst in. Julia squinted to get a better view.

"HELGA," she exclaimed. "JP—is that you?"

"Yep. We're here to rescue you. Oh my god, Pick! Dude, tell me you're OK!"

"I'm OK, I'm OK," Toothpick said, then groaned as HELGA lifted the piece of ceiling off of him and picked him up.

"Forgive me. I'm not medically trained," HELGA apologized. "Except for removing splinters. You have one of those?"

"HELGA, look at him!" JP said. "Does he look like he has a splinter?"

"He looks like he has a fractured leg," HELGA said seriously.

"No kidding, HELGIE," JP said impatiently. "Be careful. That's my bro."

"Droney!" Toothpick suddenly said. "We have to find him."

It took a few minutes, but Julia located Droney under a beam. He was dented but OK. The impact had sent him into hibernation mode, but as soon as Julia picked him up from the ground, he stirred to active mode. "All systems go," he chirped.

"All systems go," HELGA repeated, their mouth making the upward U.

"Careful, HELGA," JP said again, watching the robot carrying their friend out of the ruined weather tower. Then after a moment, "And thanks, HELGA."

"Nice work, HELGA and JP," said Julia. Then the three humans and two artificial life forms made their way back slowly to the control room.

∩

If Aurora was now free to go where she wanted, Mars knew with certainty she would return to the lava tubes. That was her base. Only, if she was going to the tubes, how would she get back? The first thing Daisy did when they had all flown away on the Lifeboat was redesign the door to the tubes with an airlock that opened from one side only. The Colony side. What if Aurora didn't know? She wouldn't have any way of getting back inside. Not if Axel was with her. Mars had to stop Aurora before she got trapped. Also, he had to convince her that she needed to work with the rest of the Colony. She had to join everyone else. It couldn't be the Colony versus the Martians anymore. Not when their lives depended on it.

As Mars kept walking down the tunnel, he saw someone up ahead.

"Aurora? Aurora?" he called out. He turned up the light on his helmet to the highest setting.

"Mars, is that you?" she called back then began walking towards him. She seemed to be alone. Where was Axel?

When she met Mars, he saw she was carrying her helmet in one hand.

"You're OK! You know about the ash cloud, right?"

"Yeah, I heard," she said. "Everyone's going to the shelters. I saw them."

"Why didn't you go, too, Aurora?" Mars asked anxiously. "It's dangerous. You don't even have your helmet on."

"I'll be fine, Mars. I have to wait for Axel. He's gone ahead. He went to bring the Martians. We need to look out for them, too."

Mars was stunned that no one had thought about this yet. "Oh my god, the Martians! You're right. We need to save them, too. I can get reinforcements, Aurora. Come back with me and—"

"Listen Mars," Aurora said interrupting him. "It's time for you to make a decision."

"What do you mean?"

Aurora paused. "We can't go on like this anymore. This isn't a life. Being trapped underground. No one looking out for us. You just saw that now. No one was thinking about us Martians. But it's more than that. You saw what Pruitt did to me. He lied to me. He made me come to this place, and then he left me behind. When we tried to find him, what did he do? *He blew up the space station.*"

"That doesn't mean the Colony can't fix—"

"It's too late to fix things," Aurora cried. "Mars, you made a promise to me. And a promise is a promise. You said you'd get me home. Well, now you have to decide whose side you're on. You saw how Orion locked us up. He's going to lock up the Martians, too. It's us or them."

"But it isn't about two sides," Mars said desperately. "That's why I came to find you, Aurora. We have to work together. The Colonists and the Martians have to—"

"I don't think so, Mars," Aurora interrupted, shaking her head. "I'm sorry, but I have to get to the airlock. Axel will be waiting for me."

"Come with me to the emergency shelter," Mars pleaded. "It's not too late."

Aurora smiled, and it reminded Mars of the first day of sixth grade in Ms. DeTemple's English class, when they completely rearranged their teacher's desk. Aurora had smiled at him then, too, and it had marked the beginning of their friendship. Now everything was different, even her smile, which was laced with sadness. "Goodbye, Mars. Thank you for coming millions of miles to rescue me. No one else would." Her voice caught at the end.

Before Mars could respond, she turned around abruptly and ran down the tunnel.

"Aurora!" It was the last thing he said before the tunnel in front of him collapsed, blocking his view of her.

26

AFTERMATH

Near the elevators, Caddie and Daisy found JP, who was leading the group back from the weather tower.

"Caddie!" JP said. "Glad you're here. Pick's hurt. He needs attention."

Caddie searched Toothpick's face. "My sense tells me he's going to be OK. But he needs medical help. Daisy, is there a team on hand for him?"

"We have a triage unit set up in the shelter right now," Daisy said. "HELGA can transport him in the elevator. We've been avoiding using it so far, but there haven't been any issues. He can get to Shelter C a lot faster than if we take the stairs."

"OK, HELGA, take Toothpick down in the elevator," Caddie said.

"I'll go with him," Julia said immediately. "Is there a charging station there, too?"

"Yes. And while you're recharging, please assess the food situation for us," Caddie said. "Daisy, what's the total count in the shelters now?"

"Four hundred eighteen souls accounted for," Daisy reported. "All healthy." She glanced at Toothpick. "Only one injury. A few scrapes and bruises, though."

"Excellent," Julia said. "HELGA, let's go. Droney, you, too. You can help me tabulate our food supply."

"There will need to be an adequate balance of shelf-stable proteins and starches, along with fresh and freeze-dried vegetables, fruits, nuts, and legumes," Droney said.

"That's my Droney," Toothpick murmured as the group entered the elevators.

"Now what?" Daisy asked JP and Caddie after everyone else had left.

"Let's figure out what else is not working," Caddie said. "Three of the generators are down, there's no oxygen in most of the upper tunnels. And Orion is still missing, isn't he?"

"Julia said she saw him fueling his shuttle," JP said. "We tried him on the IP phone, but he isn't picking up. Maybe he flew off somewhere."

"But he didn't log his trip!" Daisy burst out. "That's so unauthorized. Wait until Mr. Pruitt finds out!"

"Um," JP said. "Why do I think that won't be happening soon?"

Daisy sighed. "You're right. Since we don't even know where Mr. Pruitt is."

"At least Julia and Pick held off the ash cloud," Caddie said. "That's a huge plus. And we still have the control room. Is there anyone else we haven't heard from?"

JP frowned. "Yeah . . . where's Mars?"

FROM THE PODCAST

15 ▶ 30 ⩕⩔⩕⩔⩕⩔⩕⩔⩕⩔⩕⩔⩕⩔

Hi, podcast people. Daisy Zheng again.

So, the ash cloud is held off. Woo-hoo!

But we still have no power,

the greenhouse is destroyed, and

the food supply won't last forever.

And we kinda haven't heard from Oliver Pruitt.

Mr. Pruitt—if you're out there . . . if *anyone* is out there,

HELP!!!!

2100 Comments ⌃

andromeda   25 min ago
the colony is dying :(:(#howitends

la_girl   25 min ago
So is earth #toomuchrain #LA_is_under #howitends

allie_j   20 min ago
Wasn't mars gonna do something?? #howitends

staryoda   15 min ago
Can we mail food what's the address

galaxygenius   12 min ago
Duh we can't send anything it takes 6 mo!!! #howitends

zheng_family   9 min ago
Daisy darling, we are going to sue Mr. Pruitt!

daisy_does_good_deeds   1 min ago
I forgot to mention mars is missing too #sendhelpNOW

Axelizer   1 min ago
Haha ur in 4 a surprise #haha

27

THIS IS THE NEW ORDER

Daisy was trying her best. After all, she was Daisy Zheng, face of the Colony! Working next to Caddie had gotten her neurons firing. She even started to feel a surge of her sunny optimism return. But after she got back to the control room and recorded a new podcast (what else should she do while she waited for Caddie and JP to find Mars?) doubts began to creep in. Seeing that comment from her mom and dad was hard. They were so proud of her, and now they wanted to blame Mr. Pruitt. Wasn't he the one with the mission? Weren't kids like her going to lead the way?

The control room door flew open.

"A-axel!" Daisy stammered. "Aurora! What are you doing here?" She watched them barge in, as Axel leaned over one of the monitors, clicking wantonly on the keyboard. Both he and Aurora were in space suits, but their helmets were missing. "You really shouldn't do that," Daisy murmured.

"It's OK," Aurora said calmly. "He does that. It's not your problem, though."

"It isn't?" Daisy asked slowly. Instinctively she took a step back.

Aurora leaned against the desk where the podcast equipment rested. She was still wearing her awful space suit with the skulls-and-bones etchings. "Hmm, talking on that podcast?" she asked. "That must be a drag—telling everyone how Oliver Pruitt screwed up big time with his so-called mission. That the Colony is taking a dive."

"Um, actually . . ."

Axel came up, leering over the podcast mic. "Lookie, Aurora, it's me, I'm Oliver Pruitt. I'm your biggest living nightmare!"

"It's a good thing we found an alternate tunnel to get back in since the airlock was blocked," Aurora said. "And you know which airlock I mean, Daisy, because you probably ordered it built to seal off the Martians."

"You were stealing Colony equipment," Daisy said indignantly.

"And that really bothers you. You're so in love with this colony, even if it's a pretty one-sided love, because what has the Colony ever done for you?"

"The Colony is at the frontier of innovation, powered by kids who—"

"Stop quoting the user's guide," Aurora cut in. "I think that's what drives me so crazy about you. You're like a cookie that Oliver Pruitt baked in his Pruitt Prep bakery." She signaled to Axel. "I think we need to tell Daisy it's time to take a break."

Axel loomed over Daisy. "Yeah. Time to take a break." He guffawed on the word *break*.

"But I don't understand." She looked nervously from Aurora to Axel.

Aurora leaned forward into Daisy's face. "It means we're taking over, Daisy," she said. "Say hello to your new boss. Me."

⌒

"These space suits are so annoying," JP said, following Caddie down a tunnel. Caddie had made them first stop in the space suit room, where she checked her gear, and JP loaded up on more oxygen. "You think they could add some ventilation. I'm sweating bricks."

"We *have* to wear them," Caddie said. "When Daisy and I were looking for Colonists, we didn't have them on at first. So many of the tunnels are damaged. I don't think we can keep—" Caddie stopped.

"What, Cads? Are you getting one of your feels?"

She was frowning. "Mars . . . he's up ahead."

"Then let's go! Awesome job, Caddie!"

Their boots clomped along the tunnel ground.

"This way," Caddie said, veering to the left.

At the end of the tunnel they came to a sign that said TO WEST DOME AIRLOCK.

"Daisy showed me a map before," Caddie said. "We're really close to the surface. That must mean the oxygen is low here. I hope he's OK."

They didn't have to walk much longer. At the end of the tunnel they came to a small fork. One path led to the surface. The other led to the airlock newly built to seal off the Martians. And that's where they found Mars pacing back and forth frantically in front of a heap of debris and crumbled compound.

"Mars, are you OK?" JP cried.

He ran up to them. "I'm fine, but the tunnel just caved in in front of me, and Aurora is on the other side! I think she's trapped."

"Yikes, what?" JP asked. "What's she doing all the way out here?"

"She wanted to save the Martians," Mars cried. "Guys, we didn't even think about them! I feel so bad. And now I don't even know if she's OK. What if she's trapped under the rubble on the other side? I've been calling out her name, but there's no response."

Caddie spoke up. "I don't think she's there, Mars. I don't sense her. She's good at blocking me out, but I can still tell when she's around. My instinct tells me she's gone ahead."

"But how will she get back? This way is blocked!"

JP rested a gloved hand on Mars. "Aurora can handle herself. She'll be OK."

"She's not," Mars said. "She won't be."

"JP is right," Caddie said. "I know you want to help her, Mars, but now isn't the time. We have to get back. The ash cloud isn't going to be held off forever."

"Oh my god, I forgot!" Mars said. "Julia, Pick—are they OK?"

"They diverted the ash cloud for now," Caddie said. "Pick's injured, but he's OK—he's got a medical team on him. Daisy's back at the control room. We won't know how bad the Colony is until we contact Pruitt Prep. We have to go back, Mars."

"But I can't leave without knowing if Aurora is OK." Mars let out a big sigh. "When did it get so complicated? I mean, wasn't the Colony supposed to be this place where we solved all the problems people made on Earth? With the environment? With each other? Now the environment is turning on us. And so is everyone."

"Look, it's because Pruitt's in charge," JP said. "He's

never been for anybody but himself. If we had a better leader, we wouldn't have all these problems."

"Or maybe we can't run away from our problems," Caddie said, "just because we're on a different planet. We have to solve them no matter where we are."

"Yeah, Cads," Mars said. "I think you're right."

"Hey, Mars, your suit is blinking," JP said.

"My suit?"

JP pointed to Mars's chest, at a tiny, blinking red light on the front section of his suit.

"Whoa," Mars said, surprised. "Am I running out of oxygen? Is the suit about to explode?"

JP looked carefully. "It's a button, Mars. I think you should press it."

"Is that a good idea?" Caddie wondered.

They all looked at one another.

Then Mars pressed the button.

Mars! Greetings! A voice came from Mars's space suit.

"Oh my god, it's Pruitt," JP said. "In your space suit."

"*I'm* in my space suit," Mars said.

"It's a recording. Shhhh," Caddie said, waving them to be quiet.

"I know you might be listening to this recording in dire circumstances. In which case, the answer to your problem is at the Old Colony."

"Your *problem*?" JP asked. "Which problem does he

mean? The lack of power? The lack of food? Or heat? How about the lack of an adult figure to call the shots? And oh, boy, how about—"

"JP, wait, I want to know what the Old Colony is," Caddie jumped in. "Isn't that important?"

"The Old Colony is where it all started," Mars said. He paused. "And if that's where I have to go, then I will. Maybe that's the only way to save Aurora and the rest of the Colony."

"But how?" Caddie asked. "Where is it?"

"Right though the West Dome airlock," Mars said. "You just passed it now. It goes to the surface. I'll be able to see the Old Colony from there. Plus I've got GPS on my IP phone."

"Mars, the tunnel in front of you just collapsed," JP said. "Aurora is MIA, and there's a monster ash cloud threatening to kill us. You suddenly get a recording from Pruitt and you think it's *safe*? Don't go, bro. It's a trap."

"JP is right." Caddie shivered. "It doesn't sound right."

"Are you feeling anything, Cads?" Mars asked.

She shook her head. "Recordings don't give me any feelings."

Mars took a deep breath.

"Listen, I'll be OK. I've got plenty of oxygen." With that, Mars started down the tunnel.

"Mars!" Caddie and JP hurried to catch up. At the end

of the fork, they came to the West Dome airlock and saw Mars reaching for the seal.

"You don't have to go out there, you know," Caddie said quickly.

"I think I do," Mars said.

Caddie bit her lip. Was there no way to stop Mars?

"Wait," JP said. "I'll go with you."

"Are you sure?" Mars paused. "I think you should stay and—"

"I'm done staying. You did that once when we were leaving Earth, Mars. You're not doing that again. It's my choice. Where you go, I go."

"JP, I don't know what to say," Mars said.

"Don't say anything," JP said.

Caddie was torn. She knew it wasn't safe on the surface. Hadn't a lava bomb already destroyed the weather tower? And injured Toothpick? How would Mars and JP manage up there without any equipment or Daisy to navigate? Meanwhile, Caddie felt the tug of something else pulling at her in the other direction.

"I'm sorry, but I have to stay," she said. "The Colonists and Daisy need me. We have to make sure they're OK—that they have enough food and power to get them through the night."

"That's also really important, Caddie," Mars said. "They're

relying on you. You should go back. Just be careful. There's a lot going on under the surface, too."

Mars and Caddie paused to look at each other. Their faces were partly obscured by the visors on their helmets. Mars had grown in the last six months, and for the first time he seemed taller than she was. Or did natural disasters, even on Mars, make everything feel and look different? Around them the tunnel walls suddenly shook.

"Will I see you soon?" Caddie asked.

Mars swallowed. The truth was that he didn't know. And she could tell what he was thinking.

"You'll always see me," he said. "And JP, too."

JP fist-bumped Caddie. "Totally, Cads. We're a team."

In just the short time Caddie had been at the Colony, she had changed everything. She had helped Daisy find the missing kids, and she had taken care of so many people, including Mars. What would he do if he didn't see her back at the Colony?

"You will," she said softly, sensing his thoughts.

"Hurry, Caddie, you better go," Mars said.

She gave them each a small smile. Then Caddie was gone.

"Ready, JP?" Mars asked as he turned the seal.

JP adjusted their helmet. "Lead the way, bro."

Server: ad_astra
Sender: daisy_does_good_deeds
Recipients: colony_peeps
Timestamp: 1920 hours

Hi Colony Peeps,

Holy moly, I regret to inform you that the Colony has been taken over by hostile forces, aka Aurora and Axel! Don't visit the control room, avoid speaking to them, and PLEASE, whatever you do, don't listen to the podcast!! It is totally unauthorized what they're going to do. Hopefully you're safely in the emergency shelter. Please, only one microwave death-star chocolate brownie per kid. And be sure to recycle all glass and paper goods (bins near the door). And if you can't do the recycling stuff, don't worry. Because we're in too much trouble now anyway.

Yours faithfully,
Daisy

Daisy Zheng
Colony Chief of Communication (CCC)

♁

From the West Dome airlock, Mars and JP reached the sur-
face in minutes. The short tunnel leading up was
surprisingly clear and intact. Outside, it was early dusk
as a thin light scattered over the ochre-colored terrain. In
the distance a haze hung on the horizon. Was that the ash
cloud? And the outline of the demolished volcano? It was
hard to tell. In the other direction, they could see the faint
outline of the Old Colony. And in front of them was an endless stretch of rolling red ground.

For a moment JP felt tears springing to their eyes. "It's
so empty," they breathed. "I dig it, but honestly, it's kind
of scary."

Mars nodded. "It's your first time, right? The emptiness.
The vast unknown. Like encountering our own humanity,
our puny insignificance in the universe."

"Mars . . ." JP's voice struck low.

"Don't worry, you'll get used it."

"Not that," JP whispered. *"Look!"*

There in front of them stood two fearsome tardigrades.
In unison, the creatures lunged toward JP and Mars, their
bellows shaking the Martian air.

28
AFTERSHOCKS

The elevator lobby had been ransacked. There was graffiti scribbled on the walls, and the sign announcing CHEF SURPRISE IN THE DINING AREA had been shredded to bits. Everywhere Caddie looked, items were torn, thrown, or broken, lying abandoned on the floor. Camera monitors were smashed, doors to the bathrooms and kitchen areas kicked in, and in front of the cafeteria a mysterious pink liquid that smelled like pink-lemonade concentrate oozed on the floor.

It looked like a storm had swept through, but Caddie knew what was going on. She could feel it. The rage of children suddenly left free to roam as they pleased. Not happy, well-fed children, but hungry, dirty kids who had turned to creating havoc as a way of erasing the darkness that had filled them for weeks and months.

"The Martians," Caddie murmured. Then she saw

them, tearing down the halls, whooping, gleeful, unstoppable, children no older than herself. Some of them were in space suits, many were not. There were at least two dozen, underfed and uncontrollable kids.

"Stop running," she called out, worried for them. "You don't understand—there isn't enough air here. The more you run, the faster you'll run out of oxygen." But her warning went unheeded.

She hurried to the control room, dodging several Martian kids who bolted past her.

Inside, she was in for a rude surprise.

"I'm so sorry, Caddie," Daisy said tearfully. "I tried to stop them."

There she was, the missing Aurora, now sitting with Axel at the head of the command module. A generator had been started, and the video monitors were blinking pell-mell on the walls. On the screens, Martian kids could be seen running up and down, terrorizing each other. There were half a dozen in the kitchen raiding the refrigerators and ice chests.

Aurora looked up. "Caddie," she said casually. "You're back. Axel, start up the podcast, will ya? We've got a special message to shoot out to planet Earth."

Caddie's mind was agog. "So *this* was the plan all the time?"

"You got it," Aurora said. "We're now in charge."

"But everything is gone," Caddie said incredulously. "The greenhouse, the weather tower, the laboratories. The East Dome is shattered and now a hazard zone. We have literally *nothing*. You're squandering one of our last generators. For what? A power grab?"

Aurora's eyes narrowed. "You're trying to read my thoughts, aren't you? Well, it won't work. You can't do that with me."

"I don't want to be in your head," Caddie said.

"I don't think you could handle it," Aurora shot back.

Caddie's eyes flickered to Daisy, who was getting worked up, seeing Axel flicking on the podcast station unceremoniously. "Like I told you before, that's going to reach millions of kids," she told him anxiously. "You have to be careful. Because they'll . . ."

"Stuff it, Daisy," Axel growled. "You think I'm stupid or something?"

"You're not stupid," Daisy said. "Just maybe a tiny bit hasty?"

"Listen, Aurora," Caddie said. "I'm not going to let you do this. I'm not going to let you jeopardize the lives of hundreds of kids here."

Aurora gave a brittle laugh as the lights above them started to flicker.

"What are you going to do to stop me?" she asked.

FROM THE PODCAST

This is Axel. We're taking over the Colony.

That's right: the Martians are in charge!

We never liked this podcast anyway.

Now we're gonna cause major DISRUPTION.

Allie-j, you're a whiny loser.

Galaxygenius? You sound pretty *stupid* to me.

And neptunebaby? You *are* a baby.

Welcome to a new order.

Comment if you're with me for:

total anarchy

do what we want,

bring down Oliver Pruitt

and all the stinking Colonists.

Yeah!!!

---

356 Comments ⊗

andromeda   25 min ago
i'm gonna be sick #howitends

la_girl   25 min ago
U suck axel #fightback

neptunebaby   20 min ago
U totally suck axel #fightback

galaxygenius   15 min ago
Axel someone's gonna come kick ur ^%$^#

destructive_comet   12 min ago
I'm with axel #anarchy #sickofearth

zheng_family   9 min ago
Consider yourself sued too, Axel.

allie_j   5 min ago
Where's daisy?? #fightback

29
IN THE OLD COLONY

"Run!" JP yelled. "We have to get away!"

"No, wait!" Mars said. "I know what to do!" He looked around and spied the egg-shaped rocks scattered along the West Dome perimeter. "Here, here." He took a few and threw them at the largest tardigrade. Tartuffe opened his mouth wide.

"There you go, boy," Mars said. "Here's another, Tartuffe. You, too, Emi! Attagirl!"

JP watched, flabbergasted, as Mars fed the tardigrades one by one.

"You mean these monsters are . . . pets?" they asked. Even inside JP's space suit, they could feel their skin crawling. Nothing in the size, shape, or teeth suggested that these huge things were friendly.

"Not pets," Mars said. "They were created in a lab at Pruitt Prep and somehow they ended up here. We use the tardigrades to move boulders and equipment. At first I was scared of them, too. I have a tranquilizer in my boot that I'm supposed to use if they're about to kill me."

"Do you have it now?" JP cried. "Maybe now's a good time to use it!"

"Yeah, but look at them. We're fine. Tardigrades are pretty smart. And they like these sodium nitrate rocks. They're full of salt, I guess. So I use the rocks to get them to do stuff for me." Mars looked around. "That's strange. Where's Duke?"

"You had time to befriend a bunch of mutant tardy-spiders?" JP asked. They grinned. "I have to hand it to you, Mars. OK, rocks, not darts. I can vibe with that. Here, hand me a few."

For the next few minutes, JP and Mars fed the tardigrades, and the only sound was the creatures' jaws crunching up the stones. When they were done, they stared at Mars thoughtfully.

"They seem to dig you," JP said. "But now what? I thought we were going to the Old Colony."

"Yeah." Mars entered the name into the GPS on his IP phone. "Whoa. I didn't realize how far away it is. The Old Colony is an hour by foot. I'm not sure we have that much time. Or oxygen."

"Maybe forget going. I mean, when has Pruitt ever told the truth?"

Mars was looking up at Tartuffe. The creature was bending down, its head at Mars's level. It growled, but it wasn't a scary kind of growl. Mars edged closer and closer until he was in touching distance. A wild idea came over him. But was it his idea? Or Tartuffe's?

Mars said, "I think I know a faster way to get to the Old Colony." Then without saying anything more, Mars mounted Tartuffe.

Tartuffe responded with a gurgle and lifted his head.

"Mars! Mars!" JP called. "Don't tell me you're riding that thing to the Old Colony!"

"Why not?" Mars called back. "It's weird, but I think Tartuffe knows what I'm asking him to do. Whoa!"

JP looked at Emi, who was bending her head down, too. "Wait, Mars! Wait for me!"

JP threw their leg over Emi's neck, and then the two tardigrades charged over the landscape as the sun began to set in the distance.

∩

Nothing compared to the thrill of riding a tardigrade. Tartuffe was incredibly fast, and he seemed to glide over the rocky terrain in a way no horse could on Earth. What was even more astonishing was how Tartuffe seemed to know exactly where Mars wanted to go without being told. Had Tartuffe understood Mars all along?

JP was equally delighted riding Emi. They whooped and

hollered and threw their gloved hands in the air. "Look at me now!" JP shouted. Only at one point did JP say, "Hey, what's that smell? Did my tardigrade . . . let a big one rip?"

Mars laughed to himself. No point telling JP that Emi was the farting tardigrade.

Eventually a set of steel buildings rose in the distance. Mars knew from his GPS that it was the Old Colony. The tardigrades *had* understood where Mars and JP wanted to go. As they reached the clearing, Tartuffe and Emi strode right up to the door of the tallest structure. Then they bowed their heads and unloaded the two onto the ground.

Mars patted Tartuffe after dismounting. "Thanks," he said.

"Thanks, Emi," JP said. "Though maybe next time go easy on the beans."

"JP!"

"What? Just some practical advice, you know."

Mars was searching the door, trying to figure out if there was a button or access code when the door suddenly opened. "No way!" Mars said. "What are *you* doing here, Orion?"

"Fly!" Orion was wearing his signature orange-and-yellow space suit and helmet, the one Mars had seen on the spaceship when they were first flying to the space station. The space station that no longer existed.

"Come on in!" Orion said. "Once we go through the

airlock, you can take your helmets off. Man, am I glad you guys are here! I've been in a jam ever since I came."

"What do you mean?" Mars asked as he and JP hurried in, following Orion through the front airlock. After they got inside, Orion removed his helmet, and Mars and JP did the same.

"Boy that feels good," JP said. "Who wants to wear a trash can on their head all the time?"

"Is there enough air inside?" Mars asked.

"There's plenty of air," Orion said. "I've seen to that."

"But why are you here?" Mars asked. "We kind of need you back at the Colony. It's a total disaster. Aurora is missing and . . ."

"And, like, a whole lot of OTHER stuff, Mars," JP said, interrupting. "No power, losing air, and losing supplies because of the ash cloud."

"What about the kids?" Orion asked, concerned. "Did you find them?"

"They're cool," JP said. "Julia and Toothpick managed to stop the ash cloud, and Caddie and Daisy got everyone to the shelter."

"Everyone but the Martian kids," Mars added.

"Oh no," Orion said. "You're right. We have to look out for them, too. I'm glad that Caddie and Daisy were able to help. Look, I'm sorry I had to bail. But when the volcano went off and I heard Jonas say it was triggered, I knew it wasn't nature that set off the eruption. It was a person."

"Pruitt!" JP said. "Why am I not surprised?"

Orion nodded. "Still, I had to find out for sure. Was Pruitt responsible? When the space station blew, and he wasn't at the Colony, there was only one place left to find him. So I fueled up my space shuttle and got all ready to go. But I remembered I needed clearance from Colony Control."

"Yeah, Daisy would insist!" JP said. "She's all about rules."

"I figured she'd have a cow if I left unauthorized. So I got on Duke instead and—"

"You mean the other tardigrade?" Mars said. "You know how to ride them, too?"

"That's classified, Fly," Orion said, now grinning. "Anyway, stay with me on this. I'm trying to catch you up."

"Why are you calling him Fly?" JP asked. "Am I missing something, or can Mars really fly?"

Mars grimaced. "He just likes to *not* use my name. Go on, Orion."

Meanwhile, Orion was leading them down a passageway constructed of concrete and steel. It wasn't nearly as fancy as the elaborate carbon fiber and titanium tunnels of the New Colony, but the inside was dry and well lit.

"So Mars, you got to be ready for this, OK?" Orion said. "It wasn't supposed to be this way. We were supposed to create a new order, get everyone up to speed, and go on making new inventions, new discoveries, all that stuff. But then—something happened." Orion paused. "Now we got to find a way to make it up to the kids. Because we let them down bad."

"Orion, you aren't making sense," Mars said. "What do I need to be ready for?"

Orion looked from JP to Mars. "I don't even know how to tell you, man. I finally get it, why you're here. Why you were chosen. But you're gonna have to hear it for yourself." He stepped to one side as they entered a cavernous hall.

JP looked around them. "Where are we? It looks like . . ."

"A staging area," Orion said. "You'll see why."

Before Mars could ask what Orion meant, he heard a sound up ahead. Footsteps approaching on the cement floor.

"What in the world . . . ?" JP murmured.

The person walking toward them was tall and dressed in a white flight suit. He was not wearing a helmet. He was not a beam of light. For the first time there was no pinging sound. Then he was standing in front of all of them, face-to-face.

"So," said Oliver Pruitt. "We meet at last, Mars. You and me."

30
SECRET OPERATION

I can't believe you pushed us out," Caddie said indignantly. She and Daisy were standing outside the control room while Aurora blocked their way. She hadn't wanted them in there while Axel recorded, so they had been stuck in the dimly lit hallway of Tunnel A. "Our helmets are still inside," Caddie said. "We need them. We're losing air out here."

"Hold your breath," Aurora said unhelpfully. "You'll get your helmets back in a sec. Look, Axel needed some privacy to make his first podcast. When he comes out now, we should congratulate him!"

"What's everyone going to think on Earth?" Daisy fretted. "They're going to be freaking out about this podcast."

Aurora's eyes became slits. "I have news for you, Daisy. They don't give a rat's tail what we're doing here. That's why we have to figure out how to go home."

The door to the command room opened.

"Well, that was epic," Axel said, smirking. "I think I'm a hit. I already got like a hundred comments."

"This is such a disaster," Daisy warbled.

"Us being on this planet is a disaster," Aurora said.

The elevators opened, and out came Julia on her rover with HELGA, who was carrying a bandaged Toothpick, with Droney behind them.

"What are you all doing out here without your helmets on?" Julia asked. "You know the tunnels are depressurizing."

"Ambient oxygen levels are at sixty-percent," Droney informed everyone. "And falling."

"We need to go back inside the control room where it's pressurized," Caddie said. "How are you, Pick? Why aren't you in the emergency shelter with the other kids?"

"He insisted on coming back," Julia said as the group moved inside the control room. "He thinks he's needed up here."

"Pick, are you OK?" Aurora asked.

"That's a first, asking about someone else," Caddie said.

"Oh, my god, I'm not a monster, Caddie," Aurora said. "Pick's my friend, too."

"I'm fine, Aurora," Toothpick said. "I have a fractured tibia, but the team downstairs built a cast using leftover heat-shield material. I'll be hopping around soon enough. HELGA has been carrying me around. Thanks, HELGA."

"My pleasure," HELGA said. "My capabilities are expanding."

"They sure are," Caddie said.

"I don't get it. You fell down or something?" Aurora asked.

"The weather tower collapsed on us," Julia said.

"While they were out saving rest of the Colony from the ash cloud," Caddie said shortly. "They're heroes, unlike you, Aurora."

"Caddie, you're getting really boring," Aurora said.

"Hey, Aurora, look at this," Axel said. He held out a folder marked CONFIDENTIAL UPDATE ON OLD COLONY SPACE-CRAFT. "I thought you'd find it pretty interesting—ha, ha."

"What?" Aurora was astonished. "Is this what I think it is?"

Daisy and Julia looked at each other.

"Give me that," Julia said, lunging forward, but Aurora was too quick. She held the folder up in the air.

"That's confidential," Julia warned. "It was built entirely by kids in the Colony. A real first for them, of which they should be enormously proud. But it needs to be tested."

"What needs to be tested?" Toothpick asked.

"HELGA, do you know?" Caddie asked.

"I'm afraid not," HELGA said. "Not all files have been downloaded to my system. Especially if they originate from a paper source at Colony Control."

"No one knows about it yet, Caddie," Julia said. "Except upper management. It's a security issue. That's why it's all been stored offline."

Aurora was scanning the documents inside the folder. "It says there's a spacecraft on Mars. Not the Lifeboat or another shuttle. But the *Manu 1*, a full-range spacecraft capable of going extended distances. According to this document, it says the *Manu 1* is fully operational as of . . . last week. Oh my god. This is it, Axel!" Aurora was wild with glee. "This is it!"

"You can't possibly be thinking what I think you're thinking," Caddie said. "Julia says it hasn't been tested. Visibility is poor. There could be a second volcanic eruption."

"Caddie, we may never get another chance," Aurora said. "Oliver Pruitt doesn't care about you. He doesn't care about any of us. We're just part of some bizarre experiment. Well, it's time for the experiment to end. Look what's happened to the Colony. It's been destroyed." Aurora held up the folder. "Do you really want to be destroyed next?"

∩

"You!" JP's voice rang out across the hall. "Are you another hologram trying to confuse us? Maybe I should come over and smack my fist into your virtual—"

"JP," Mars said. "I think he's real."

"One hundred percent real," Orion said.

"JP, you should get an award for being most ready," Oliver

Pruitt said. "You certainly have all your pistons firing."

"But just because he's real doesn't mean he isn't trying to confuse us," Mars said. He paused, taking a moment to look Pruitt over. Mars couldn't help it—that strange thrill he was feeling. It was from years of wanting to meet this person, who was now standing in front of him. But Mars also knew that this thrill was the most dangerous feeling he could have. It could be the very thing that would prevent him from seeing the truth if he wasn't careful.

"First you bring me all the way to this planet," Mars said. "You make me travel for six months, and when I get here, where are you? You aren't even around to meet me face-to-face. You tell me my friends are safe on Earth. Then I find them in sleep pods on the space station, which is set to explode! Then I'm back at the Colony, and there's another explosion. Orion says it was triggered by you. Now we're running out of power, food, and . . . hope. Aurora doesn't want to be here anymore, and I don't know what to tell her." Mars crossed his arms. "So what is it, Oliver Pruitt? Why should I trust you? How do I know you won't cause more terrible things to happen?"

"You're right," Oliver said. "I haven't been straight with you. But I couldn't take the risk, not until I knew I had really created a safe place for you and everyone."

"But this place *isn't* safe!"

"Mars, Mars." Oliver's voice turned urgent. "Every day, there are threats. Leaving Earth, we left behind the needless mistakes that humans have made: climate change, pollution, congestion, population growth. It's raining right now across the West Coast, and parts of the South. Not normal rain. Torrential rain, excessive rain. The streets in California are flooding! And your beloved Washington is next."

"Wait—really?" JP asked quickly. "What about our parents? Are they OK?"

"No one can be OK for long if the same people on Earth keep being in charge. That's why it's better on Mars, because we're in charge. But threats abound here, too. Threats always abound."

"What kind of threats?" JP said. "You mean the tardigrades? Because they helped us."

"Ah, the tardigrades," Oliver Pruitt said gravely. "Let's say we have other things to deal with, JP. First of all, we can't have the wrong humans here. And they're on the way. Believe me. They want to use my space station, my colony, and I won't have them come and replicate the same mistakes they made on Earth, when everything was coming along so beautifully here."

"Seriously?" Mars asked. "You're worried about other humans coming? Aren't we already here?"

"Yes," Oliver said, nodding. "And we have to keep weeding out the bad ones—the ones who create problems, the weak ones, the ones who can't adapt."

"Weak ones?" JP repeated. Their eyes narrowed. "I don't like the sound of that."

"Not you, JP," Oliver said. "You have more than proven your worth. All of you here have. Orion is a fabulous pilot. He has shown his worth a hundred different ways. And JP, there is no one I know who is physically stronger than you."

"Then what about me?" Mars asked. "Or any of the kids at the Colony? We're not all strong. We're not all pilots. And we're not all smart like Julia or Toothpick. Are you saying we're too weak to be here? Do we need weeding? JP's right. I don't like what you're saying either."

"Oh, Mars, you're special. You've always been special," Oliver said. He came forward several steps and Mars unconsciously took a step back. "Don't you know by now? Did your mom never tell you?"

"My mom?" Mars repeated. He felt the blood from his face suddenly drain.

"You're right," Oliver said softly. "I can see from your face, you know. Maybe you have always known. You're here because you're special and resourceful and very bright. And also, Mars, because you're my son."

AHEAD OF THE CURVE

The room seemed to tilt around Mars. Like a kaleidoscope, all the experiences of the past year were colliding together for him toward this single moment. This single, terrible moment. Oliver Pruitt stood still, watching him as Orion crouched, as if expecting another explosion. JP was the one who broke the silence.

"Are you punking us?" they demanded. "'Cause this isn't *Star Wars*. So if you think you can do one of those Luke-I'm-your-father lines because it's your idea of entertainment, then you've got another—"

"JP." Mars's voice cut in. "I appreciate the backup."

"Any time, bro," JP said.

"But he's telling the truth," Mars said. "I know."

JP glanced at Orion, who nodded. "I found out five minutes before you got here. And he told me because he knew that was the only way I'd . . .well, let him tell you. But how did you know, Fly?"

"I know because it all makes sense." Mars's voice had changed. It was more strained. On the verge of tears, but still angry. "The postcards, the toy rocket you sent me in the mail for my birthday when I was seven, the way my mom acted whenever I mentioned your name."

Oliver Pruitt bowed his head. "Yes, for Saira . . . for your mom, it was very hard. Knowing who I was and not telling you."

"But why?" Mars looked away. "All those years you were gone . . . all my science fairs you missed. Why didn't you both tell me? Where were you?"

"I was here, Mars," Oliver said. "I was always keeping an eye on you."

"From where? Mars?" Mars swept his hand around. "By making your podcasts? Even then, you couldn't just leave me alone, could you? You had to keep taunting me, then visiting my school and humiliating me in front of everyone in the assembly."

"Oh, yes," Oliver smiled ruefully. "You really don't forget, do you? But I had to do it, Mars. I had to see how tough you were—if you couldn't handle the ridicule of your class-mates, how would you handle the rigor of colony life on Mars? I had to see how you acted under stress. Not as a follower, but as a leader. And Mars, you held up beautifully.

That viral video you sent me where you declared war? Brilliant! You became a hero with kids everywhere. They wanted to support you, be you, follow you. You couldn't have done any better."

"But I didn't do it to score points!" Mars exclaimed. "I did it because you threatened me and my friends. Because my mom and my friends are the only people I have. I certainly never had a father. All I had was the idea of you—the mystery of you—and that day when I turned seven and I got a toy rocket ship in the mail. That day became special because it was the *only* day. A day when it snowed. Did you know that? It was the first time I saw snow."

"Whoa, like, it *never* snows in Port Elizabeth," JP said. "But I remember that day. We got shut out of a Seahawks game."

"When I saw the snow," Mars went on, "I began to believe in miracles. That maybe I'd see you for real. Not just get a toy in the mail."

Oliver stepped forward. "But you were right to believe that, Mars," he said softly. "You *were* going to see me. I was going to be with you. I'm with you now." Gingerly he stepped forward, and Mars felt the man's arms embrace him, space suits at all.

Mars breathed in and out. Then his arms went up, and he used them to push himself away. "It's not that easy," he said hoarsely.

"That's right," JP said. "You're still Darth Vader in my book."

Oliver straightened and cleared his throat. "No. Of course it isn't easy. I don't imagine it ever will be, Mars. But I'm not Darth Vader, JP. This isn't *Star Wars*. It's your lives, and you all have to decide if you're going to live ahead of the curve or behind it—and suffer all those losses that Earth will experience in the near future. So give it some thought, JP, Orion, and . . . Mars." Oliver glanced at his watch. "In the meanwhile, we don't have time to lose. The shuttle launch is in fifteen minutes."

"Shuttle launch?" Mars asked. "What're you launching?"

"Let me guess, the Old Colony is actually a rocket ship," JP said sarcastically. "And we're your copilots."

For the first time, Oliver Pruitt threw back his head and laughed. "JP, you never cease to surprise me. So direct! So on the nose, aren't you?"

"What are you saying . . . we *are* on a rocket ship?" JP asked in disbelief.

"No," Oliver Pruitt said. "But see that door behind you? It leads to the launch pad of the *Manu 1*, a fully operational, state-of-the-art rocket craft, headed for Earth. And it's scheduled to depart in fourteen minutes."

"You mean you're leaving? Again?" Mars cried out. "What about all the kids still at the Colony? How will they survive? The tunnels are depressurized, the control room is on the blink, they're not going to be able to handle it if you're gone."

"Yes, I know you're thinking of them," Oliver said, "but with the catastrophic loss that the Colony suffered at the hands of the volcano, we can't survive without more resources. We have to go to Earth and bring back more kids. We have to bring back more equipment."

"But you're the reason the volcano blew!" JP shouted. "You're the reason for the catastrophe. You *are* the catastrophe!"

"The volcano could not be helped. Someday you'll understand there is a method to my madness. But meanwhile, Phase II is about to begin! Orion, prepare the cockpit for departure."

"Are you sure?" Orion asked reluctantly. "Mars and JP are right. We can't leave everything like this. It's a mess."

"My fellow space travelers," Oliver said. "Paraphrasing the great Japanese poet, Mizuta Masahide, sometimes you have to burn down the barn to see the moon. Orion, please prepare the launch sequence. We don't have a fancy audio countdown, I'm afraid. You'll have to trust me—we have twelve minutes left."

"But Caddie, Julia, Toothpick, Aurora," Mars said. "There are too many friends here. I'm *not* leaving, Oliver Pruitt. You can't make me."

"I can't make you," Oliver said. "But the rocket is leaving.

And soon there will be no supplies left. Come with me and live, or stay back with no guarantees."

"I can't leave my friends," Mars said helplessly. "And what about the other Colonists?"

Oliver had brought out his helmet from an alcove, and he slid it on, making his face unreadable. He cut an impressive figure. He always had. Tall, confident—Oliver was the father Mars had always wanted but never had.

"The Colonists need us to bring back more supplies and resources to rebuild the Colony," Oliver said gently. "Don't you see? They're depending on us to go back to Earth. As for your friends . . . if they were here right now, we would bring them. But the servers are down, the IP phones don't work inside here, the space buggies need to be refueled, and time is running out. Your friends getting to the Old Colony before takeoff? *That* would take a miracle."

Mars's thoughts were racing. Oliver Pruitt—his father— was always calling the shots, always controlling their destiny. Now Mars had nothing: no equipment, no weapons, and worst of all, no time. But he did have his heart and his mind. So he closed his eyes and sent his thoughts faster than the speed of light, catapulting them across the barren red landscape.

32
IT WOULD TAKE A MIRACLE

urora waved the folder in front of Daisy and Julia. "So where is it?" she demanded. "Where is the *Manu 1* being hidden? I saw you looking at each other. I know you know. I know you think you're trying to be heroic and save the Colony. But you've seen the place. We're never going to survive—not with the ash cloud coming, the tunnels destroyed, and in a few weeks, we'll run out of food. We have to get out of here."

"Droney, is that true?" Toothpick asked his drone. "Are we out of food?"

"The freezers are at full capacity," chittered Droney.

"But they will be rapidly depleted since the greenhouse has been depressurized and the ash cloud threatens to destroy it in its entirety," HELGA noted. "Lack of food in human populations can lead to low morale, starvation, death, and in some extreme cases, cannibalism."

"HELGA!" Julia chided. "Don't be gruesome."

"CPUs are repurposed frequently," HELGA said. "It's known as 'the facts of life.'"

"Listen, we have enough food to survive," Caddie said. "And we can fix the tunnels. Didn't the kids build them in the first place? We just have to work together. Aurora, you should put that folder back where it belongs."

"And reading classified information is a violation of Section 5.2 of the Colony Constitution," Daisy reproached. "You ought to know better, Aurora."

"Who cares?" Aurora said wildly. "You guys want to stay? Fine. Me and Axel, we're leaving. He's a pilot. Trained at Pruitt Prep and everything."

"I'm a killer pilot," Axel acknowledged. "'Course, I've never actually flown a spacecraft in space. But I put in my flight simulation hours. That counts."

"OK, the less said the better, Axel," Aurora said. "Daisy, Julia—you need to tell me where that spacecraft is."

"Aurora, as chief security officer," Julia said angrily, "I refuse to disclose its location, for your safety and ours. In fact, *you're* our gravest security threat right now. Maybe it's time to put you and Axel back in the service room."

As they went back and forth, Caddie had turned as pale as a ghost. She clutched her forehead and staggered. "Ow!" She yelped.

Julia and Aurora stopped talking.

"What's happening, Caddie?" Julia asked in concern. "Are you hurt?"

Caddie bent over.

"It's her headache," Aurora said. "She's getting something. A message?"

"A vision," Toothpick announced. He was still standing on one foot next to HELGA.

Caddie continued to grimace. "Julia, Daisy, you're not going to like this, but I'm getting a message from Mars."

Daisy's eyes widened. "You are? Where? Like on your phone?"

"Did you get a text, Caddie?" Julia asked, puzzled.

Caddie nodded with difficulty. "A message, not a text."

"In her head," Toothpick explained. "Caddie, for reasons unknown, reads minds."

"That's right," Julia said. "That's how she found the Colonists."

"And I know where Mars is!" Caddie jumped in. "He needs us. He needs all of us. Aurora, too. He wants us to get to the Old Colony in the next ten minutes. He says our lives depend on it. His, too."

"Well, if Mars's life is depending on ours," Toothpick said, "I don't think we have a choice. Where's the Old Colony?"

"It's all the way over on the other side of the lava tubes!" Julia said. "Are you sure? I'm sorry, but ten minutes is impossible!"

"Impossible," Toothpick agreed.

"It would take a miracle," Droney said.

"Or Orion's space shuttle," HELGA said. "It is fueled and ready to go in the shuttle station. Daisy is merely required to disengage the security bolt."

"HELGA!" Julia said. "You are simply amazing."

"Thank you!" HELGA said.

"Then let's go," Caddie said urgently. "We need to get to that platform."

"Tunnel A is the fastest," chirped Droney.

"Wait, that's it? Just like that, you're all going to the Old Colony?" Aurora called out behind the others. "But I need to find out—"

"Aurora," Caddie's voice cut in. "You'll want to come when you hear this. You know that spacecraft you were talking about? The *Manu 1*? Well, it's at the Old Colony. And it's on schedule to launch . . . in ten minutes."

33
A QUEST FOR NORMAL

ars! Mars!" JP's voice reverberated in the hall. "Are you OK? Open your eyes!"

"Hey, man, open your eyes!" Orion leaned toward him.

Mars took his hands off his face. "I'm fine. I was just thinking. I can still do that." He glared at Oliver Pruitt. "And I'm not finished!"

The man's casual suggestion that Mars's friends could stay behind possibly to die in the Colony was unforgivable. There was no way Mars was going to let his dad convince him to go along with this plan. His dad! Just thinking that made the acid rise in Mars's throat. Of all the people, it had to be Oliver Pruitt, the most despicable man in the universe. There was a time the discovery would have thrilled him. Now it felt like a curse. Maybe his dad thought he could ditch everyone like he always did. But not this time.

Not if Mars could help it. He had to find a way to deactivate the launch. He had to find a way to stop Oliver Pruitt.

Suddenly Mars remembered the tranquilizer dart stored in his left boot. It was there for tardigrade emergencies. But wasn't this an emergency, too? Mars wasn't sure of the dosage. He wasn't sure whether a serum intended for a six-hundred-pound tardigrade would kill his dad or merely derange him. But Mars didn't have time to find out. From the compartment, he removed the dart. It was like time slowed down as Mars lunged forward, hand raised. He saw his dad's mouth gape in shock—as the needle plunged into Oliver Pruitt's thigh.

⌒

Luckily, everyone was suited up, so the only thing that required time was for Daisy to deactivate the security bolt. After that, it was a quick run to the shuttle platform. As they were loading themselves onto the shuttle, Daisy hung back.

"Daisy, aren't you coming?" Caddie asked in alarm. "Mars meant you, too."

Daisy smiled bravely and shook her head. "No, Caddie. I think . . . I think I'm needed here. Remember, there are four hundred twenty Colonists."

"But . . . but Daisy," Caddie said sadly. "You can't do it alone."

A figure moved toward Daisy. "I will stay with Daisy,"

said HELGA. "I am a transit assistant, designed to make one's stay pleasant. I will make Daisy's stay at the Colony pleasant. Nothing is more pleasant than surviving!"

"Oh, HELGA!" Daisy said, smiling tremulously. "I feel better already."

"Guys—we have to go!" Aurora called out. "Remember, the clock is ticking!"

Reluctantly Caddie slipped inside as the hatch was sealed.

"I'm so glad Axel's a pilot," Aurora said as everyone strapped in. "He's so gonna get us out of here!"

"Um," Axel said, staring at the cockpit. "Where's the orange button?"

"Oh, for god's sake," Julia said impatiently. "I'll do the flying. You try not to do anything stupid, all right, Axel?" Then Julia deftly took over the controls.

Two minutes later, the shuttle roared out of the docking station. Because they didn't have to leave the atmosphere, it was just a short flight over the surface. They went up a comfortable five hundred feet past the ash cloud, with views of the Colony, Monument Crater, and the smoldering Mount Olympus peeking through the ash. In the distance stood the Old Colony, a set of massive concrete buildings rising up from the ground.

"We're coming, Mars," Caddie whispered inside her helmet. She wished she could beam her thoughts the way he had to her. It was a miracle that she had felt them all the way across the rocky Martian terrain. They were so strong the words had physically assailed her like a punch in the gut.

Caddddddie. Come to the Old Colony . . . Come to the Old Colony before it's too late.

And now the entire interior of the Old Colony was coming to Caddie, too: the steel and concrete structures, the control panels, the smooth hallways, the launch center where *Manu 1* readied for departure. And standing there, next to Orion, JP, and Mars, was the man who'd brought them all here. He was the genius, the entrepreneur, and the crazy man, and now, as he had just revealed, he was also Mars's . . . Caddie gasped.

∩

Footsteps pounded in the hall of the Old Colony. Mars was overjoyed to see everyone: Aurora, Caddie, JP, Toothpick, Droney, Julia, and even that annoying sidekick of Aurora's, Axel, who was looking dazed.

"Caddie!" Mars exclaimed. He ran to her, grabbing her arm. "It worked. You heard me, didn't you?" Just seeing her filled him with sudden strength. She was here, and now it was all going to work out.

"Oh, Mars, I always hear you," she said to him. She saw the inert Oliver Pruitt lying on the ground. "But what on earth happened here? He's not . . ." Her voice dropped.

"Don't worry, he isn't dead," JP said. "Just off to la-la land for now."

"Guys, hate to interrupt, but the launch sequence has been activated," Orion said. "I thought I could stop it, but there doesn't seem to be a way. It's leaving for Earth. So if you're gonna get on board, now's the time, folks."

Aurora shoved her way forward. "I'm getting on. Who's with me?" She stopped in front of Mars as if she was about to say something. Then she saw his hand on Caddie's arm, and she ran past them to the craft without another word.

JP stepped forward. "Pick, buddy, you gotta go back. Your leg needs some real help. Not Colony health care. Sorry, no offense. And everyone," they stopped, swallowing. "I gotta go back, too. I left my folks behind, and I've been down for the mission all this time, but it isn't right leaving my parents to think I'm dead."

There was a murmuring, then one by one, the crew boarded the spacecraft: JP, Toothpick, Droney. Orion and Caddie helped Mars drag Oliver Pruitt onto the ship. "We'll need him when he wakes up," Mars said. "Right, guys?"

"You will," said Julia, who was standing at the entry. "Because I'm not coming."

"Julia!" Mars said, stunned. "Why?"

"Me either," Orion said. "Don't worry. You'll have the autopilot until Pruitt wakes up, and then he can fly you. It's just that I gotta stay back with Julia and Daisy so we can take care of the Colonists. But you come back later for us, you hear?"

Mars looked at them with a heavy heart. "You're both awesome. Do you know that? We will restock and refuel. We will definitely come back. I promise."

Orion shook his head. "You sure like to make promises, Fly!"

"You are an amazing leader, Mars," Julia said. "We'll see you in the stars!"

"Oh, man," Mars said. "I'll miss you guys."

Orion smiled at Mars as he pulled down the hatch.

Inside the cabin, there were just two minutes left for Mars to strap himself in, secure his dad, who was still fast asleep, and prepare for takeoff. "Talk about unreal, right Caddie?"

He looked through the cabin, where his friends were strapping themselves one by one into their seats. He saw their faces, and that was when he had a terrible realization.

The engine started to roar.

"No!" Mars said, his voice drowned out by the engine. "Caddie!"

Server: ad_astra
Sender: caddiepatchett
Recipient: thisismars
Timestamp: 0800 hours

Mars,

Our server is finally up! Julia reconfigured the system and HELGA helped. You must know by now that I'm not on the spaceship. It was a hard choice. I wanted to stay with you. Honest. But the kids here need my help. They don't have many people to help them rebuild the Colony. But with Daisy, Orion, Julia, and HELGA, I think we can. I'll learn how to find tunnel leaks and plug them up. And how to find those sodium nitrate rocks you were telling me about to keep the tardigrades happy. And there's so much more to learn, too. The Colony isn't perfect, but it's ours. And I'm counting on you guys to come back and see all the changes we've made. All of you. Maybe even Aurora, if she changes her mind about this place. I miss you, Mars! But this isn't goodbye forever. Just for now.
To the stars.

Yours,
Caddie

∩

Once the *Manu 1* had left Mars's atmosphere and reached outer space, the autopilot kicked in and the spacecraft began cruising toward Earth at a constant speed. The expected travel time was six months and three days. There was a notable sigh of relief as everyone took off their helmets and space suits and put on one of the flight suits found in the mid-deck. It was also time to microwave a few snacks and settle back.

Even so, Aurora was already complaining. "I've got, like, nothing to do. This sucks."

After a few grudging minutes, Axel and JP began playing gin rummy while Toothpick studied a manual that would teach him how to upgrade Droney's circuits. Meanwhile, Oliver Pruitt was sitting up, still groggy, in the cockpit. The sleep serum had finally worn off, and he had been allowed into the flight cabin because technically, he was the only one who knew how to fly. Axel's flight-simulator hours didn't count.

"What a doozy," Oliver mumbled. "Good thing you didn't get me in the jugular. I might really have been down for the count."

"Don't tempt me," said Mars, who was sitting next to him in the cockpit and watching over the flight screens. He was making sure that his dad didn't get any weird ideas, like commandeering the ship and rerouting them to Jupiter. Oliver Pruitt was capable of anything.

As Mars sat in front of the monitors, he couldn't stop thinking of Caddie, about the choice she made to stay back at the Colony. How did she make such brave decisions and always put others before herself? She was the real leader. Not him. Not Aurora. And now even Aurora knew that, too. She had tiptoed around him on the space shuttle, trying to be nice, like letting him use the microwave first for dinner. Only once did she mention Caddie to him when she said, "I guess you miss having your mind read." Other than that, Aurora steered clear of Mars. Maybe it was better that way.

Now Mars had to find a way to go back and see Caddie again—and everyone else who had stayed behind. A promise was a promise.

☊

A few minutes later, JP sauntered into the cockpit. "OK, out, Mars. It's my turn for lookout duty," they said.

Mars got up, bleary-eyed. "Thanks, JP. I think I'll crash for a few minutes in the crew cabin."

"Sounds good," JP said. After Mars left, they turned to Oliver Pruitt, observing him coolly. "Looks like our fearless leader is awake. I bet you can't wait to brighten my day with your witty self."

JP settled themself breezily at the control monitor.

"You don't look like a pilot," Oliver Pruitt said. "And yet

you presume to be operating a spacecraft. I must still be dreaming."

"Stuff it," JP said. They stared at the monitor. "I know how to look a screen. See here? We're on autopilot. For six months. How hard can that be to understand? Except . . ." JP pressed a button several times. "What happened to the signal from Pruitt Prep?" They leaned forward into the microphone. "Come in, Pruitt Prep Mission Control."

Oliver glanced at them. "What's the problem now, JP?"

"You tell me. You got a clue why the signal isn't working?"

Oliver leaned forward. His eyes were bloodshot from the serum, and his voice was still slurry. "Of course the signal is working," Oliver said irritably. "Because Pruitt Prep Mission Control is . . ." He stopped. For a moment he tried several switches, then he tried rebooting the monitors. His voice grew hoarse as he spoke into the microphone repeatedly. "Pruitt Prep—can you read me?"

At last, there was no mistaking it.

"What?" JP said. "Am I right? See? I told you. Why aren't we getting a signal from Pruitt Prep? Is their signal missing?"

Oliver shook his head. "It's not the signal that's missing," he said thickly. "It's *Earth*."

FROM THE PODCAST

This is Daisy Zheng from Colony Command Central.

I've got some special guests with me. Woo-hoo!

Tell us, how safe is the Colony?

Julia: It's never been safer!

Orion: We've got protocols, right, Daisy?

Daisy: Absolutely! And our Colony is being rebuilt.

Caddie: And don't forget, we now have a school!

Daisy: Let's say it, everybody!

All: To the stars!

877 Comments ⊗

andromeda   40 min ago
Hurray daisy!!! #howitbegins

staryoda   40 min ago
I heard you can raise chickens on mars #farmingonmars

allie_j   31 min ago
I heard you can grow trees on mars #forestsonmars

galaxygenius   23min ago
I heard you guys are gonna be okay #howitbegins

neptunebaby   15 min ago
If this is how it begins then

Daisy banged repeatedly on the keyboard, her monitor blinking an error message. She turned around.

"Guys," she said in dismay. "We've lost them."

ACKNOWLEDGMENTS

Space travel requires a mission-control staff, technicians, engineers, flight specialists, trainers, and personnel on the ground. Writing this book required just as much guidance, and I couldn't have done it without my team of experts. A universe filled with thank-yous goes to Benjamin Strouse, Chris Tarry, David Kreizman, Jenny Turner Hall, and the cast and crew of the original podcast series *The Unexplainable Disappearance of Mars Patel* who were the ones to first envision this intrepid mission. Special stars are to be given out to my brilliant team at Walker Books US: Susan Van Metre, Lindsay Warren, Maria Middleton, Phoebe Kosman, Anne Irza-Leggat, Maya Myers, Maggie Deslaurier, and all the other incredible members continuing to support the launch of this exciting interplanetary project. Thank you to Frances Clair, for her insight and knowledge on the subject of Friedreich's ataxia. Thank you to Marietta Zacker and Steven Malk, two brilliant stars in the agent galaxy. And the artwork featured on the covers of these books is breathtaking and out of this world; thanks to our highly esteemed illustrator, Yuta Onoda.

Lastly, thank you to Suresh, Keerthana, and Meera for traveling through space and time with me. You are cherished.

ABOUT THE AUTHOR

SHEELA CHARI is the author of *Finding Mighty*, a Junior Library Guild Selection and Children's Book Council Children's Choice Finalist, and *Vanished*, an APALA Children's Literature Award Honor Book, an Edgar Award nominee for best juvenile mystery, and a *Today* Book Club Selection. She has an MFA from New York University and teaches fiction writing at Mercy College. Sheela Chari lives with her family in New York.